Brody's Pledge

Brody comes to Brentwood Falls in Arizona Territory to keep a pledge made at his mother's deathbed, to avenge the wrong done to her, years earlier. Befriending town sheriff Will Tasker, and catching the eye of beautiful singer Louise Delaware, Brody is a man of wealth, yet prefers a life of manual labour, and accepts employment shoeing horses in the town smithy. Before long, Brody has made enemies of his mother's nemesis, rancher Dan Slaydon and his wastrel son. He also faces the enigmatic outlaw known only as Ishmael, whose motives are as mysterious as his real identity. Brody and Tasker will find their courage stretched to the limits before Brody's pledge can be fulfilled.

Brody's Pledge

Alvin Ford

A Black Horse Western

ROBERT HALE

ISBN 978-0-7198-2791-4

The Crowood Press
The Stable Block
Crowood Lane
Ramsbury
Marlborough
Wiltshire SN8 2HR

www.bhwesterns.com

Robert Hale is an imprint
of The Crowood Press

Typeset by
Derek Doyle & Associates, Shaw Heath
Printed and bound in Great Britain by
4Bind Ltd, Stevenage, SG1 2XT

CHAPTER ONE

The stranger joined the stagecoach bound for Brentwood Falls at Silver Springs. There were already two other passengers, an attractive young lady and an older gentleman, who had been en route from Tucson. They sat facing each other. The new passenger sat down beside the older man.

The newcomer offered his hand to the gentleman, and said, 'My name's Brody. Er, John Brody.'

A person meeting Brody for the first time might estimate his age at about twenty-five, although he was older than that by almost a decade. He was slim but muscular, five feet nine inches in height, and carried himself with an unconscious ease, but that could instantly switch to decisive action if the circumstances demanded it. He kept his face clean-shaven. His head of dark-brown hair was luxuriant and thick, and he wore it unfashionably long, although not long enough for drunken cowhands to even think of calling him 'sissy' in a saloon. In any event, people's attitudes to tonsorial style had changed since the death and subsequent fame of the late General

Custer, and Brody had found that fewer people made remarks since the newspaper reports of the Little Bighorn.

The other man grasped Brody's proffered hand and shook it vigorously. He said, 'Bradford Stillman. Delighted to know you, Mr Brody. I have a law practice in Brentwood Falls. I'm just returning from a bit of business in Tucson.' He let go of Brody's hand, and gestured towards the lady. 'This is Louise Delaware, star and co-owner of the Majestic Theatre, the town's main source of entertainment.'

Brody turned to Miss Delaware, nodded, and offered his hand. Miss Delaware grasped it delicately with her silken-gloved hand.

'An entertainer?' Brody said. 'An actress, perhaps . . .'

'I can act,' she said, 'but we don't have a big enough company to put on plays. We mostly put on singing revues, and I'm the singer.'

'I hope I can come to see your show while I'm in Brentwood Falls,' Brody said.

After these introductions, the passengers had little in the way of conversation. Stillman seemed deep in thought, and Miss Delaware passed the time reading the new book by Mark Twain, *The Adventures of Tom Sawyer*, which had been published the previous year. Brody thought to mention that he had met the author a few years earlier, but refrained from doing so, not wishing to sound boastful after such a short acquaintance and kept his own counsel. Brody was also unwilling to talk about his reasons for travelling to Brentwood Falls, and didn't wish either of his travelling companions to become too curious. Brody, however, had a natural curiosity about most people he met, and in other circumstances would have been eager to enquire politely about their lives.

The lawyer noticed that the newcomer hadn't said anything about his reasons for travelling to Brentwood Falls, but kept his own counsel about whether this reticence indicated some kind of malign intent or otherwise.

Stillman was a man of maturity, nearer seventy than sixty, and was of middle height. He was handsome enough, but had never married, although that wasn't from lack of interest in, or from, the ladies. His hook nose sat between green eyes that had a slight downward cast, and his thin lips seemed permanently pursed, almost on the verge of turning into a scowl, but that didn't stop the more mature ladies of the county from regarding him as a fine figure of a man, and more than one of the town's widows had offered him friendly attentions with the hope of a marriage proposal, but none had ever been forthcoming.

His hair, currently concealed by a derby hat, was thick and curly and had mostly turned grey over the years, and his hairline had receded somewhat since his youth. Despite his age, he had never considered retiring from the law, although he had sufficient funds in the bank should he wish to do so, but there was plenty in the town to keep him busy. In any case, he doubted whether his most important client, Dan Slaydon, would allow him to retire.

Miss Delaware appeared to be concentrating on her book, but she cast an occasional glance at the handsome stranger, and, like Stillman, wondered about the young man's intention in travelling to Brentwood Falls.

She was about thirty but had been a professional singer and dancer for several years, and looked as trim as a girl half her age.

Her pale-blue dress was exquisitely-tailored, and daringly low-cut and also provocatively short, allowing a glimpse of her ankles. Her matching bonnet had a ribbon which tied under her chin. The outfit was complemented by a matching jacket for outdoor and travelling wear. She carried herself proudly, aware of admiring gazes of the male sex, but her manner projected a dignity and composure which meant that men rarely overstepped the bounds of propriety.

After the stage had travelled for about an hour, a rumbling sound began in the distance, like continuous thunder. Brody looked out of the window and saw a cloud of dust rising behind them. He shouted out to the driver, 'It looks like somebody's chasing after us.'

'I hear it,' the driver shouted back.

The shotgun messenger reached reflexively towards his weapon. He said, 'I don't like the sound of that, Gus.'

The driver, Gus Dedman, said, 'Me neither, Curly.'

'There hasn't been much trouble in these parts recently.'

Gus glanced backwards. 'Keep an eye on it. A couple of barrels of buckshot usually scares off Indians or bandits.'

Inside the coach, Stillman fingered his holster nervously. Louise stroked her face lightly, seeming a little paler despite the rouge on her cheeks.

The thundering got louder as the chasers got closer.

Brody looked out of the window again and said, 'Bandits, it looks like. I reckon there are four or five of them. They're catching up.'

Dedman pulled at the reins to make the horses run faster. They were still a good distance from the next staging post, and he reckoned the bandits would catch them long before they reached it, but nothing would be gained by making it any easier for their pursuers.

Curly reached for his weapon, a standard-issue short-barrel shotgun loaded with buckshot. A blast at short range would do a deal of damage to anybody who thought a stage would be easy pickings. The risk of death and injury was enough to dissuade most outlaws. Curly turned around so that he could get a shot at the pursuers and waited. While there was no worry about aim, he knew that the chasers had to get near enough to hit them.

'Damn,' said Dedman. 'There's more of them up ahead. We're not going to be able to outrun them.'

'What's the option?' Curly asked. 'Surrender?'

'Maybe if we go fast enough we'll get past the ambushers.'

The trail led into Black Rock Canyon, with reduced room to manoeuvre. 'We can't get around them, but if we're going fast enough they might not be able to stop us.' Dedman flicked his whip to get the horses to speed up. They were still fresh and responded easily.

Curly was worried, however. He could take aim at the pursuers or the ambushers, but not both, and there was no protection against gunfire from the ambushers.

Inside the coach, Brody said, 'I've got experience in these matters. I've worked on stagecoaches before. Six months as a shotgun messenger, and five weeks as a driver. Wells Fargo didn't like it much when I handed in my resignation. I'd prevented three stages from being robbed, one of them when I was the driver.'

'How interesting,' Louise said.

Brody opened the door and climbed onto the roof of the coach. He slipped into a position behind the driver and told him of his experience with stagecoaches.

'That's mighty helpful,' Dedman said. 'You armed?'

'Just a handgun. Colt Peacemaker. Full belt of ammunition. More ammunition in my baggage, but that would be hard to access in a hurry.'

'We've got a spare shotgun,' Curly said. 'You can use that.'

The coach charged on. Brody took up the extra shotgun. To Curly he said, 'You take the ambushers. I'll go for the chasers.' Then he lay down on the coach roof, with some cover afforded by the baggage, and took aim at the pursuing riders.

The trail narrowed as it went into a valley, hills rising above it on both sides, and the track became rougher. The coach began to jolt up and down, which made Brody's aim more difficult. The coach neared the ambushers, and Gus urged the horses to keep going flat out. The five bandits in front were aiming rifles at them. Dedman pulled at the reins even harder, urging the six horses to keep charging forward. On the uneven ground of the trail, the coach bounced up and down more than usual, its straps straining with the motion. Curly took aim with difficulty, and fired, but a wheel went over a small rock as he did so, and the shot was knocked to one side, so only hit one of the bandits.

The pursuers were coming up fast, two to the left, two to the right. Brody took aim at those on the right, holding it, waiting for them to get a bit closer. Then he fired.

One of the two was hit. The other's horse was hit, and he jumped from his saddle as his mount went down.

Brody shouted to Curly, 'Any more ammunition?'

'Down in the compartment beside me,' Curly said.

Brody reached down, picked up two more cartridges, and reloaded. He shimmied back into position and took aim at the two riders on the left flank. They were getting nearer and had begun to ride slightly further apart.

Brody took aim and fired. He clipped one pursuer, who fell from his horse.

A shot boomed behind Brody. Curly screamed, and fell from the coach, dropping his shotgun as he did, so that it fell on his seat. Brody knew that he would have to give up on the pursuing rider, and went to take the shotgun seat. He grabbed Curly's shotgun, still fully loaded, and raised it to bring it to bear on the ambushers.

Another slug whizzed past his ear, and a groan issued from Dedman.

'You all right, Gus?' Brody asked, not taking his eyes off the aim along the short barrel of the shotgun.

'I'm hit. I think my shoulder's busted.'

Dedman had lost all strength in his left arm and was now unable to hold the rein, which flopped down at his side. The horses on the left slowed, but he was still pulling at the other rein, and those horses continued to charge on. The differential speed caused the coach to lurch, and begin to turn leftwards, off the trail.

Brody grabbed for the dangling reins, attempting to get the left side horses back on track, but it was too late. The coach had left the track, and was riding up a slope, causing all the horses to slow.

There was no chance now of escaping the bandits. Brody reached over and brought the coach to a complete halt. He hopped down from the seat, opened the carriage door, and slipped inside the coach.

'Is everybody all right?' he asked.

'I am,' Stillman said. 'Miss Delaware?'

'Me too,' she said.

'Curly was hit and fell off the coach. I don't know if he's dead. The driver has been hit too, slug caught him in the shoulder.'

'What do we do now?' Stillman asked.

'I think we'll just have to let ourselves be robbed,' Brody said ruefully.

The pursuers caught up with the coach, dismounted, and approached with guns outstretched.

Brody glanced out of the window. He saw that they were wearing bandannas over their mouths, which he knew was a good sign, because they were trying to conceal their identities. Had they been showing their faces, there was more chance of being killed.

One of the ambushers approached the coach, and said, 'I'd be very obliged if you would get down from the coach. Please. And no sudden movements.'

The door opened.

'Nice and easy.' The bandit raised his gun. 'Keep your

hands where I can see them.'

Stillman stepped down to the ground

'Away from the coach, please,' the bandit instructed. 'Walk slowly towards my colleague just over there.' He gestured to his right. 'He's going to frisk you.'

'I'm not armed.'

'I can't take your word for that.'

Stillman allowed himself to be frisked.

'This one's clean, boss,' the outlaw said.

'OK,' the boss said. 'Let's have the lady out here now.'

Louise moved to the coach door, and delicately stepped out.

'Well, aren't you the fine-looking woman?' the bandit said. 'I'll be frisking you myself.'

'Why don't you leave the young lady alone?' Brody appeared in the open door-frame and scowled.

'Why don't you just mind your own business?' the outlaw snapped back.

'You don't look so tough,' Brody said. 'You look like a coward to me.'

'You don't look tough to me at all, mister,' the outlaw said. 'You'd pull a gun on me this instant if you thought you wouldn't get a bullet in the belly. But my friend over there . . .' he motioned to where another outlaw had a rifle pointing at Brody '. . .he will fill you with lead if you try anything.'

'Big man,' Brody said. 'Needs somebody else's gun so that he can talk the brave talk.'

'Get down here so we can frisk you. Is your name Stillman?'

'No, it isn't.'

'Then the other man must be Stillman.' The outlaw took a step toward the coach and looked inside. 'OK. Very slowly, walk towards my colleague.'

Brody moved closer to the other outlaw who began to pat him down.

Suddenly, there was a crack like a thunderbolt.

The outlaw abruptly let go of Brody, stiffened, and fell to the ground. Brody turned and looked down at him and saw a bullet-hole in his back. The outlaw chief peered around in alarm. A shot whizzed above him, catching his Stetson and causing it to fly from his head. He dived towards the coach, to gain some cover. Swiftly, Brody drew his gun, approached the bandit, and pressed its barrel against the man's left temple.

'I don't think that I will be getting frisked today,' Brody said. 'Or robbed.'

'Certainly looks that way.' The bandit no longer looked so cocky. Brody pulled the bandanna from his face. He could see now that the man had mean, thin lips, and a prominent, jutting chin.

'Do you recognize him, Mr Stillman?' Brody asked.

'No,' Stillman said.

The other bandit still had his gun pointed at Brody, and said, 'You can just put that gun down right now, mister, or I'll shoot you.'

Brody laughed. 'I don't think so,' he said. 'My finger is very firm on this trigger, and if you hit me my finger will spasm, undoubtedly killing your boss here.'

'That's very true,' the outlaw leader said. 'Hank, drop your gun.'

Hank began to argue, but his leader interrupted. 'Do

as the man says.'

Hank's face twisted in a scowl, but he dropped his gun to the ground and raised his hands to the heavens.

Brody turned his gun away from the boss man and shot Hank in the belly.

'What?' the outlaw said. 'What did you have to go and do that for?'

Brody immediately turned the gun back towards the outlaw and pressed the barrel to his head again. The outlaw winced in pain from the heat of the newly-fired gun. Brody said, 'I didn't like him. I like you, though, which is why I'm not planning to kill you, even though you're a no-good bandit like the rest of them.'

'Decent of you.'

'It won't stop me taking you to Brentwood Falls and handing you over to the sheriff. And I hope you get a fair trial followed by a good hanging.'

'Much obliged for the appreciation.' He seemed unconcerned at the reversal in his fortunes.

'What's your name?' Brody asked.

'Call me Ishmael,' the outlaw said.

'A wise guy, huh,' Brody said. 'Literate as well as criminal.'

'What's he on about, "Ishmael"?' Stillman said. 'That's from the bible.'

'Yes, first son of Abraham,' Brody said. 'But it's also a character in a novel by Herman Melville.'

'Never heard of him,' Stillman said.

'And you an educated man, too,' said Brody. 'I suppose there's not much time for reading novels in law school.'

'Nor for a career outlaw either, I would guess,' Stillman said.

Ishmael scoffed. 'You'd be surprised, Mr Stillman.' Then he cast his eyes towards Brody and said, 'I'd be obliged if you'd not press the barrel of your gun quite so hard against my head. It's making me nervous.'

'Good,' Brody said. 'You should be nervous. Would you tell us why you were holding up the stage?'

'To rob you.'

'I don't think so,' Brody said. 'You're altogether too interested in Mr Stillman. You knew he was on this stage coach and set out to get him. What for, I can't figure out. What do you think, Stillman?'

Stillman said nothing.

'Am I right, Mr Ishmael?' Brody asked.

'Can't rightly say,' Ishmael said. 'Like I told you, we were just out to rob you.'

A figure came stumbling along the trail, kicking up dust. 'It's Curly!' Louise shouted out and ran towards him.

Brody turned to look and saw Curly walking unsteadily towards them. He had lost his hat and the sun was reflecting from his bald head. His clothes were covered in blood.

'Glad to see you're not dead, Curly,' Brody said.

'How's Gus?' Curly asked.

'In the excitement I forgot about him.' Brody looked up at the driver's seat, where Gus was clutching his side. 'How are you, Gus?'

'I think I'll live this time,' Gus said. 'Although I wish I'd taken up farming like my wife suggested. Is Curly all right?'

'Still among the living, at any rate,' said Brody. 'How are you, Curly?'

'I think I'll probably live this time,' Curly said. 'I see you managed to overpower these ruffians, thanks to me shooting one of them.'

'I wondered who'd done that,' Brody said. 'Good man. You'll be getting to ride inside the coach for a while. I'll take on the driving, at least till we get to the next staging post. Meanwhile, we need to tie these *ruffians* up.'

Brody thought for a moment, then said, 'Stillman, I'm going to take my gun away from Ishmael's head so that I can get the rope. Can you make sure he doesn't try anything?'

Stillman nodded and pressed his gun at Ishmael, not at his temple, but in the belly.

Brody went to the coach's stowage compartment, being familiar with the style of the coach, a Concord Stagecoach manufactured by the Abbot–Downing company in their factory at Concord, Massachusetts. He knew their vehicles well from having worked on them. He swiftly located a rope and a knife and cut four shorter lengths of rope.

'Do you know how to tie knots?' he asked Stillman.

'No, I don't.'

'Just as well that I do, then.' Brody expertly tied Ishmael's hands. 'That'll do for just now. I'll tie your feet together when we get into the coach.'

'Neighbourly of you,' Ishmael said.

Brody quickly tied the other bandit, pushed him over to the coach, and bundled both men into the compartment. With ease he tied their legs together, immobilising them.

17

Brody said, 'I'll drive to the next staging post and we'll see what happens when we get there.'

'Would you like me to ride in the shotgun seat?' asked Stillman.

'I think I'll be all right on my own.'

'What are you going to do about the dead bandits?'

'Going to have to leave them for the vultures, unfortunately. If we risk collecting them and bringing them along, it will delay us further. And if they have confederates that Mr Ishmael hasn't told us about, we could end up in big trouble.'

Having ensured that all the others were safely aboard, Brody climbed up to the driver's seat and got the stagecoach back on its way.

As he drove, he hoped that the quirk of destiny that was bringing him to Brentwood Falls wouldn't be as troublesome as this hold-up. But he doubted it. This might just be the beginning of his troubles.

CHAPTER TWO

Sheriff Will Tasker sat outside his office, a vantage point from which he could watch the main street. He rocked in his chair, keeping a lookout for anything out of the ordinary.

The stage from Tucson had been due around noon, and it was now over two hours late. He was a bit concerned but it was too early to organize a search party. Stages were often late, but the delay was rarely longer than an hour or so. He would worry about that later if the stage didn't turn up.

He had been sheriff of Brentwood Falls for over a decade. Carrying his fifty years lightly, he looked considerably younger. He stood six feet two inches tall, weighed two hundred pounds, but was lean and muscular. His piercing-blue eyes were hooded by his bushy eyebrows. His nose was aquiline, slightly bent where it had been broken in a fight some years earlier. His ears seemed slightly too big for his head, not that anybody would dare remark on it. He had a firm jaw, and was clean-shaven, being meticulous about keeping his chin smooth, shaving himself every morning, except on a Monday, when he went down the street to Bart Badger the barber, who gave him a hot towel shave. In earlier years as sheriff, he had worn a moustache to give an impression of maturity. But now that he was older, he had no need of this, and his fiancée had complained of itching from his chin.

He had been a deputy in Silver Springs and moved to Brentwood Falls when invited to become its sheriff. It was officially an elected post, but the town mayor had asked him because there were no other candidates.

He heard a sudden commotion from the saloon, and stepping off the boardwalk in front of his office, he loped across the street to investigate.

He got half-way when the saloon's batwings flew open, and a figure was abruptly catapulted from them. Tasker recognized Rick Slaydon, son of the owner of the Triple S Ranch. No surprise there.

Rick Slaydon was aged twenty-five, had red curly hair, and his face was a mass of freckles. He was short and lean, almost skinny, and had a snub nose. He was always trying to grow a beard to make himself look older, but the hair on his chin and upper lip always remained wispy and fluffy, and the effect only made him seem more youthful. His manner and demeanour were more like those of a spoilt fifteen-year-old rather than a grown man, and most of the townsfolk dreaded his frequent visits.

Rick lay sprawled in the street and groaned loudly. After a few moments, he partially recovered his senses, and pushed himself up onto his knees. He looked dazed, not from having been thrown bodily from the saloon, but because he was drunk.

No-good Slaydon kid, always getting soused and causing trouble, thought Tasker.

'Wha . . . Where . . . Wha. . .' the boy babbled. Tasker filled a bucket from the nearby water trough and threw the contents over Rick.

'Ricky, always causing trouble,' Tasker said.

Rick shook his head, vainly trying to shake the water off as it ran down his neck. 'Lea' me 'lone, Sheriff.'

'Sorry, Ricky, can't do that.'

'Why not?' Rick mumbled.

'You're drunk.'

'Not drunk. Jus' wanted to have drink, play little poker.'

'You're too drunk to play poker. If you were a bit less drunk, I'd put you on your horse and send you back to the Triple S. But you might fall off and hurt yourself, and your pa would blame me. I'm going to have to put you in a cell until you sober up, or your pa comes to get you.'

There was a sudden look of fear in Rick's eyes.

'Not tell my pa,' he said.

'Then I'll have to keep you in jail all night. Your pa will come looking for you, and I'll get the grief.'

'Not tell my pa,' Rick repeated.

'We've been through this before. Your pa will want to know where you are. I'll get a load of grief if I don't send word to him.'

'Not tell my pa!' Rick was whimpering now.

Tasker knew this could get messy.

'Not tell . . .' Rick drew his revolver and pointed it at the sheriff.

'Ricky, don't do that.' Tasker wasn't afraid—

Rick was a terrible shot, even when he was sober. Rick fired at Tasker, but the bullet went through the window of the sheriff's office.

'That's enough now, Ricky,' Tasker said, and was on the boy in an instant, seizing his wrist and squeezing it so that he would drop the gun, which fell harmlessly into the dust. This had to stop, right now, because although Rick was unable to hit anything on purpose, he might do more damage. He could have shot one of the townsfolk instead of just a window. It had happened before, but Rick always got away with it because of his father's position in the county.

Rick sobbed. Tasker twisted the boy's arm behind his back, then grabbed the other arm and pulled it around too. Holding both wrists easily together in one hand, he turned Rick around and pushed him across the street to the sheriff's office. Benjy Britton, the deputy, scratched his grey beard, and stood aside as Tasker pushed Rick through the open doorway.

'Thought you were a goner for sure that time, boss,' Benjy said.

Tasker scoffed. 'He'd have to put a bullet in my brain from point blank range to hit me, and he'd still probably miss.'

'Bullet came through the window and nearly hit me.'

'Good thing you're so short then, Benjy,' Tasker said. 'Put this lad in a cell. No need to lock it. Pour as much coffee down his throat as you can, sober him up.'

'Sure thing, boss.'

'I'll go over to the saloon, see if there's anybody from the Triple S there, tell them that Rick's working off his drunk in jail, and that his pa can come for him if he wants.'

Benjy took Rick by the arm and led him through to the cells, and Tasker turned to go to the saloon.

Just as he was about to step off the boardwalk, the overdue stage pulled up in front of him. Squinting his eyes slightly because of the afternoon sun, he saw that the driver was unfamiliar to him, and was dressed not at all like a stagecoach driver, but like a doctor or a professional gambler.

'Are you Sheriff Tasker?' the driver asked.

'Sure am. I take it there's been some trouble with the stage.'

'That's right. My name's Brody, and I'm one of the passengers.'

'What happened to the driver?'

'He's inside the coach, being looked after by Miss Delaware. He's injured. We were held up by bandits.'

'What about the shotgun messenger?'

'His injuries were worse, so we had to leave him at a staging post, where the operators sent for a doctor. I hope he's going to be all right. If it hadn't been for him, we might not have been able to get the better of the bandits.'

'What about the bandits?' Sheriff Tasker asked.

'We killed or injured seven or eight of them. Hard to say exactly. We lost count. We captured two of them. We've got them tied up in the coach.'

'Is it Gus Dedman who's the driver?'

'Yes. I'm sure that he'll be all right, but he needs medical attention.'

'The passengers all right?'

'Yes. None of us were harmed. There are only three of us.'

'Anybody aboard that I would know? You mentioned Miss Delaware. What about the other passenger?'

'Mr Stillman mentioned that he's a local. You know him, of course?'

'Indeed, I do. I often have dealings with him. He's the only lawyer in town. I'll be wanting to speak to all of you later. There's a bit of business I have to attend just now in the saloon. But my deputy will look after you while I see to that.'

Sheriff Tasker crossed the street to the saloon, and found Tom Durden, one of the Triple S ranch hands, and told him what he had done with Rick. He asked him to inform Slaydon. Durdon looked none too pleased but agreed to go back to the ranch at once to tell the boss what had happened.

Then Tasker headed back over to his office to see what was going on. Stepping inside, he saw that Benjy had locked up the would-be robbers. Dedman was sitting in the sheriff's chair. Brody was attending to him, loosening a tourniquet.

Brody said, 'Benjy told me that the doctor would come if we sent a messenger. So, I asked a little boy nearby to run fetch him. I told him that I'd give him a dime if he brought him back within ten minutes.'

Tasker nodded. 'Doc Stephens will be here soon, I'm sure. You might as well disembark the coach right here. Its proper destination is the hotel, which is just over the street, right there next to the saloon. I know where I can find Miss Delaware and Mr Stillman when I need to talk to them. I presume that you'll be staying at the hotel.'

'That's right. By the way, it was agreed at the staging post where we dropped off Curly, that I would act as the coach driver until we reached our destination. I was told that I should leave the coach and the horses at the livery stable until the coach company can arrange for a replacement driver and shotgun messenger.'

The sheriff said, 'You'll find the livery stable further along the street, towards the edge of town. Big sign outside says *Sumpter's Livery Stable*. Ask for Tex Sumpter. You can go there when you're done disembarking the coach.'

'I'll do that. Then I'll come back here and give you a sworn statement.'

'No hurry. These prisoners won't be going anywhere for a while.'

'That's what you think!' came a shout from the cell corridor. Brody turned to look and saw that it was the taller of the two prisoners, the one who called himself Ishmael.

He was grinning broadly, as if he hadn't a care in the world.

CHAPTER THREE

Tex Sumpter was making the rounds of the livery stable, tending to the horses that were being stabled there for the night. His apprentice was taking care of the feed and that the horses were all getting settled.

Tex had firm features, although nowadays slightly jowly, suggesting a man who had been once lean and handsome. His lips were turned down slightly, as if in a permanent scowl, but he had brown eyes and thick, bushy eyebrows, and his twinkling eyes contradicted the impression of a frown. He was aged about sixty, and felt every year of it in his bones. He walked with a limp, the result of an injury that he had sustained during the Civil War. Prior to the war he had been a ranch hand, but his injury had made him unsuitable for such work since then, and he came to Brentwood Falls to work in his uncle's livery stable. He had later inherited it after his uncle had died in 1870.

Tex was facing a problem, but not at the livery stable. Five years ago, he had acquired the blacksmith shop next door, and was worried that he might now have to close it up. Ned Bateman, the blacksmith who operated the smithy for him, had been killed the previous week by accident. There had been an argument about a poker game in the saloon, and shots had been fired. Everybody knew that the gunman was Rick Slaydon, but nobody dared to testify against him for fear of his father's wrath. Ned hadn't been involved in the game, but had been hit in the chest by a ricochet, and although he had lived for three days after the wounding, Doc Stephens hadn't been able to save him. Denny Radley, Bateman's fourteen-year-old apprentice, had only just started learning the trade, and while he was fairly competent at smithing, he hadn't been taught anything of the art of the farrier. Everybody in the county who knew the trade was already employed. So, horse-shoeing, the main stock-in-trade of the smithy, wasn't currently possible until the vacant position could be filled.

Tex saw a stagecoach approaching and was surprised to see it being driven by a man dressed like an easterner, and was even more surprised when it came to a halt in front of the livery stable.

'You Tex Sumpter?' the driver asked.

'I am,' Sumpter said.

'The sheriff said I would find you here. My name's Brody. Er, John Brody. You'll have guessed from my clothing that I'm not a regular coach driver. This is the stage from Tucson. We got held up a distance after Silver Springs. The driver and the shotgun messenger both got injured, but we managed to get the better of the bandits.'

'That's the coach Gus Dedman drives. He all right?'

'Doc Stephens is going to be looking after him. We

had to leave the shotgun messenger . . .'

'That would be Curly.'

'That's right. We had to leave him at a staging post. But the company representative there agreed that I could drive the coach the rest of the journey rather than face delay. I told him that I'd worked a few years back as a coach driver, so they agreed to do it. They said that I could leave their horses at your livery stable. The stage-coach won't be able to make its return journey until they arrange for a replacement driver and messenger. So, here are the horses. Have you room to accommodate six?'

'Sure. Normally I'd ask for some money in advance . . .'

'The stagecoach company said they would reimburse you. I know that they have an office here in town. I passed it on the way here.'

'Good of you, Brody. I've room for the six horses. You can park the coach around back, and we'll unhitch the horses.'

'One of the horses felt a little sluggish the last few miles or so. I think it might have gone lame. Hoof probably needs some attention.'

'Now that could be a difficulty,' Sumpter said. 'I'm joint-owner of the smithy next door, but my business partner got killed by accident last week. His apprentice can do the smithing, but I've got nobody who can shoe a horse or look after their hoofs.'

'Well, as a matter of fact, I've got some experience as a smith and a farrier.'

'I'll be darned. I thought from your get-up that you

must be a lawyer.'

'Well, I do have a law degree, but I don't practise. I've worked at a lot of trades. Can't seem to settle at anything, though. It's not the work, I don't mind that. I just want to move on and try new things.'

'Well, I could let you use the smithy if you want to have a look at that horse.'

'Might as well. After we've unhitched, I can take it around to the smithy and have a look.'

'Sure thing,' Sumpter said.

Brody took the lame horse from the back of the stable while Sumpter was getting the other five settled. He led it to the smithy, introduced himself to Denny, then took off his coat, undid his tie, and loosened his vest. He looked around for the farrier tools. Everything seemed to be in order. All the equipment needed for the care of hoofs, and the tools for shoeing. Then he went to the horse, gently patted its neck, and raised the leg which seemed to be lame.

Sumpter came out of the livery stable and walked over to Brody to see how he was proceeding.

Brody said, 'Shoe's a bit loose, that's all. Might be a bit of hoof damage underneath, but I won't know until I get that shoe off.'

He selected the tool which would unbend the nails, straightened them and pulled them out. He tossed the nails into a nearby bucket, inspected the shoe, laid it down on a nearby bench, and then examined the hoof.

'Hoof looks fine to me. Last farrier was a little bit careless, shoe wasn't on quite tight enough.'

Sumpter said, 'You know what you're doing.'

'Yes. Lot of practice. I was apprenticed with a farrier for about six months.'

'Why didn't you stick at it? There's demand for it everywhere in the territory.'

'Just got bored.' Brody gently hammered the new nails into place, then took the clinchers and pulled the nails tightly to the shoe.

'Well,' said Sumpter, 'I'm impressed. And you're good with horses.'

'When I was first apprenticed, I got kicked by a horse that I was shoeing a rear hoof. That was a painful lesson. And I got bitten by another horse when I was working its front feet. That taught me to treat them with respect.'

Brody put the clinchers aside and examined his handiwork. 'That'll do very well, I think. You can add the cost of that to your livery bill for the stagecoach company.'

'What about paying you, Mr Brody?'

'No charge. I just did that because I could.'

'I insist.'

'In that case you can pay me the going rate.'

Sumpter rubbed his chin. A thought had occurred to him.

'Something on your mind?' Brody asked.

'I don't suppose that an educated man like you would be willing to work for me as a farrier.'

'I don't mind manual labour. I've worked at a lot of things in a lot of places. I wouldn't mind at all. In fact, I'd be happy to do it. Part-time of course, and I really don't know how long I'll be in town. Maybe two or three weeks. Perhaps longer. I can do the horse stuff, and I can do a bit of smithing if there's too much for your apprentice boy. How about I work mornings, eight o'clock until noon? Sundays off, of course.'

'Fine by me,' said Sumpter. 'Would you agree to ten dollars a week?'

'I really don't need the money, but it wouldn't be right to work for you and not expect something in return. It's a deal.'

Brody held out his hand, and they shook on it.

'I'll start in the morning. That all right with you?'

Tex nodded.

'I'll also be looking to hire a horse. I take it that you have horses for hire.'

'Certainly do. I'll show you them tomorrow and you can pick one out.'

'I'll be here.'

An hour later, Brody walked into the sheriff's office to make his deposition about the stage hold-up.

'Evening, Sheriff,' he said.

'Mr Brody. Everything settled with Mr Sumpter and the livery stables?'

'Definitely. He even offered me a job in his smithy.'

'Really? Doing what?'

'Smithing and shoeing horses.'

'You are a strange one, Brody. You dress like an eastern gentleman, but you do manual work.'

'I've done a lot of things in my time. I told Sumpter I'd worked as a farrier, when he told me that he couldn't shoe one of the horses. So, I did it, and he offered me a position.'

'Just like that, huh?'

'Don't be fooled by my appearance. I went to Harvard to please my mother. Got a law degree. But I told her I didn't want to practise as a lawyer. I took the bar exam in Massachusetts, but I've never even worked in a law office. I've done lots of things. Ranch hand; cattle and horses. I was even a shepherd for a couple of months at a sheep ranch in Missouri. Coach driving and shotgun messenger, which is why the stagecoach company allowed me to take over from the injured driver. A bit of railroad conducting, didn't like that much though. And I've been in law enforcement. Sheriff's deputy. Even sheriff of one town in Wyoming, but that only lasted two weeks before I had an argument with the town mayor and quit.'

'Never met anybody like you, Brody.'

'I'll take that as a compliment, Sheriff. I'm here to give my deposition about the stage hold-up.'

'Since you're a lawyer and a sheriff, I'll let you write your own deposition.'

Tasker took pen and ink from a cupboard shelf, and some paper from the shelf below, and then placed them on the desk nearby.

'Take a seat, Mr Brody. Take as long as you like.'

Brody sat and began to write. He had filled most of two pages in a neat and confident hand, when an imposing man barged through the door. The figure was followed by another man, who stood a pace behind him.

Brody looked up at the big man. He was tall – Brody estimated that he stood six feet two inches – and looked mature, perhaps aged sixty or older. He had piercing-blue eyes, firm lips, and a square jaw. His chin jutted out slightly and had a prominent and slightly asymmetrical dimple. His hat covered his head, so Brody was unable to tell if he was bald or not, but his grey sideburns were clearly visible, and he had big ears, the left ear a little larger and set slightly higher on his head than the right ear. His blue eyes were also a bit lopsided, with his left eye perhaps a quarter of an inch lower than his right eye. But there was nothing comical about this – his stare was cold and mean.

The sheriff spoke, 'Good evening, Mr Slaydon. You got my message.'

'I did. You've got my boy here in the jail?'

'Only for his own protection. He got drunk in the saloon . . .'

'I heard what happened. Tom Durden told me.'

'I asked him to do that,' Tasker said. 'I knew that you'd want to be informed as soon as possible.'

'I rode into town with Durden here as soon as I heard.'

Brody looked at the man standing behind Slaydon. This man wasn't as tall as his boss, a shade under six feet, dressed like a ranch hand. He was sporting a fresh black eye.

Slaydon spoke again. 'I'm none too pleased that my boy has been locked up as a common criminal.'

The sheriff rose from his seat. 'He's not locked up. He's in a cell because he needed to lie down after Benjy gave him about a gallon of coffee to try to sober him up. But the cell door was never locked.'

'Glad to hear it.'

'I talked to the witnesses in the saloon. I don't think any of them want to press charges.'

'Charges?' Slaydon spluttered. 'Charges? If there are going to be any charges they'll be brought by me. Durden told me how my son was thrown bodily out of the saloon. He could have been injured.'

'He wasn't,' said the sheriff.

'He could have been. I'll be bringing charges against the saloon owners, Mr Rutherford and that Miss Delaware. I'll be speaking to Brad Stillman in the morning, you can be sure of that. And I'll want you to arrest Rutherford and that . . . tramp for assault.'

Brody spoke up. 'Miss Delaware never assaulted anybody. She wasn't even in the saloon at the time.'

Slaydon glared at him, angry at being interrupted.

'Who the hell are you?' he asked. 'Your face seems familiar. Do I know you?'

'I doubt that. I just got into town this afternoon, on the Tucson stage. Miss Delaware was a passenger on it.'

'What of it?'

'When I came into town, I came straight to the sheriff to report the hold-up . . .'

'What hold-up? What are you talking about?'

'The stage was held up by a gang of bandits. They injured the coach driver and the shotgun messenger, but we gave them better than they gave us, and two of them are in custody right here just now.'

'What's that got to do with me? What nonsense are you talking? Sheriff, who is this idiot?'

The sheriff was about to answer, but Brody spoke first. 'Name's Brody. Er, John Brody.'

'What do I care what your name is? And why do you think I should be interested in your opinions?'

34

'It's just that Miss Delaware was in the coach when I came into the sheriff's office, and your son was already here in protective custody after the incident. So, Miss Delaware couldn't have assaulted your son, because she wasn't there.'

'Shut up!' Slaydon shouted angrily. 'Who do you think you are, speaking to me like that? What has any of this got to do with you? I don't like you, mister.'

And I don't like you, thought Brody.

'Who is this man, and what is he doing in here?' Slaydon asked the sheriff.

'He's a witness to the stage hold-up, and he's writing out his deposition against the two outlaws we have locked up here . . .'

'You've got my son in with bandits?'

'No. They're locked up in the other cells. And your son's not locked in.'

Slaydon scowled, and stepped towards the cells, found his son, and opened the door. Grabbing Rick by the wrist, he pulled him from the barred cubicle. The boy looked cowed and let himself be dragged.

'I'll take care of him now,' Slaydon said. 'You'll be hearing from Mr Stillman tomorrow.'

'I've no doubt that I will,' Tasker said.

The old man and his son went out, followed very swiftly by Durden.

'I take it that Mr Slaydon is a big noise around here,' Brody said.

The sheriff nodded. 'Yep. This would be a decent town if it wasn't for him and his people. His son is the cause of most of the minor trouble in the town, and some of it not so minor, but the old man won't see it. Bank robbers are less trouble than Ricky Slaydon.'

'You had any bank robbers lately?'

'Not while I've been sheriff here.' Tasker stroked his chin. 'I think you might have made a serious enemy there, the way you argued with him.'

'I've met bullies like him before.'

'He likes to throw his weight around. I try not to argue with him. But his son is a wild thing. Causes trouble just about every time he comes to town.'

Brody pondered. 'Perhaps the old man will keep him at home for a while.'

'I hope so. These bandits I've got locked up are much less trouble.'

'Speaking of which, I've finished writing my deposition. Would you like to read it before I sign it?'

'I'll read it tomorrow. I'm sure that with the statements I got from Mr Stillman and Miss Delaware, that will be enough to arrange a trial. So, we just have to wait for the circuit judge to hit town.'

Brody signed his deposition with a flourish.

'I think I'll go and sample the hotel's bill of fare. What with all the excitement, I didn't have time for dinner at a sensible hour. And now that I'm the town's new farrier, at least for a short time, I've got an early start in the morning.'

'Goodnight, Mr Brody. I hope that you find this town to your liking.'

'It should be all right, if I can stay out of the way of Slaydon.'

CHAPTER FOUR

Sumpter watched Brody hard at work in the smithy, almost unrecognizable from the eastern dandy who had arrived just the day before.

He wore denim pants and a work shirt, with heavy-duty boots, a functional vest rather than the dressy one he had worn yesterday, and a leather apron to protect him from the heat of the furnace. He was hatless, but Sumpter saw a cream-coloured Stetson on a peg on the wall, very different from the black derby hat of the previous day.

Brody was absorbed in the work. He had hot iron in the furnace, held by tongs, turning it molten so that he could shape it into a horseshoe. He lifted the metal from the flames, placed it on the anvil, picked up the hammer, and deftly moulded the hot metal into the required shape. When he had it the way he wanted it, plunged the metal into cold water so that it would lose its heat and stay in shape. Steam issued from the bucket, and Brody lifted the horseshoe out of the water, placing it on a metal shelf for it to cool.

Tex wondered how long Brody would stay on. He was

more skilled than the late Mr Bateman, and it would be difficult for Tex to find anybody else. Perhaps Brody would stay long enough to teach Denny the trade.

People stopped by and watched the new man at work. In the summer, the doors of a smithy were always open, so it became a focal point. Young boys, especially, liked to hang around and watch a smith at work. Sumpter used to shoo them away in case they got too close, but now he let them watch. He hoped that at least one of them would want to take up the trade. It wasn't so many years ago that Denny had been one of those lads, so keen that it wasn't just the summer days when he hung around the shop, much to the annoyance of Miss Summers, the schoolteacher. But it had been obvious that Denny had no interest in school, and that a trade would be better for him than the reading and figuring. Miss Summers had a talk with Denny's mother, and they agreed that he need not stay on at school, provided he apprenticed himself to the smith. Denny had been overjoyed and devoted himself to learning blacksmithing. But the late Mr Bateman never let him near the horses. Bateman had always said that working with hot metal was one thing and working with horses was quite another. Bateman would have come around eventually and started teaching the kid how to look after horses' hoofs, but for the unfortunate accident with Rick's stray bullet.

Tex became aware of movement behind him. Before he could look, he heard a dreaded voice shouting at him.

'Well, lookee here. You got a new blacksmith, Tex, and you still ain't re-shod Dandy.'

Rick Slaydon. Talk of the devil. If not for the boy's

father, Sumpter would have whipped the young trouble-maker years ago. But he didn't dare say anything. It was just asking for trouble.

Rick had little in the way of decency, but he did care about his favourite horse, whom he had named Dandy, and liked to keep the horse in perfect condition. In order for this to happen, strictly speaking a horse had to be re-shod every six to eight weeks. Tex knew that many of the people of the county tried to skimp on this, often stretching to three or four months. But Rick was very particular and brought the horse to the smithy every six weeks for his hoofs to be re-balanced. Unfortunately, Ned Bateman had suffered his fatal 'accident' the day before the work was due to be done. Sumpter had agreed to stable Dandy free of charge until the work was completed.

But here was Rick, having lost patience, wanting the work done now, but Brody was trying to catch up with all the other work that had been left incomplete.

'Rick,' Sumpter said, 'you know we'd have worked on Dandy last week if you hadn't shot my blacksmith.'

'Never shot nobody.'

'That's as may be. Bateman was a good blacksmith, and he's dead with your bullet in him.'

'Never shot nobody.'

'Then why did my blacksmith die?'

'Never shot nobody. Ain't my fault the idiot got in the way of a bullet.'

'I'm not going to argue with you. If you come back tomorrow, we'll have the work done.'

'Not tomorrow. Now.'

'Come on, Rick. It's my new man's first day. And he's only working part-time. I guarantee that we'll have it done for noon tomorrow.'

'Not tomorrow. Now.'

Brody looked up from the anvil. 'My, you do have a habit of repeating yourself.'

'Huh?' Rick said.

'Not tomorrow. Now.' Brody mimicked the squeak in Rick's voice. 'Not now. Maybe not even tomorrow if you keep on arguing about it.'

'Who the blazes are you?'

'You saw me in the sheriff's office yesterday evening. I was writing a deposition.'

Rick looked puzzled. 'Can't be. Guy doing that was an eastern dandy. You're a reg'lar blacksmith.'

'I can be a *regular* blacksmith when I please, or a farrier . . .'

'Huh?'

'A farrier shoes horses, a blacksmith works metal.'

'Huh?'

'Do you not understand American? Did Noah Webster live in vain?'

'Huh?'

'*Habla Espagnol*, perhaps?'

'Huh?'

'Doesn't speak Mexican either. *Parlez-vous Français?*'

'Huh?'

'Huh? Not French? How about *Loquerisne lingua latinam?*'

This time Rick just looked vacant.

'Somehow I didn't think he would speak Latin.'

'Cut it out, Brody,' Tex said. 'There's no need to make a fool out of the boy like that.'

'I don't like him. He's ill-mannered, and ignorant. Didn't like his father either.'

Tex stepped closer to Brody, speaking softly so that Rick couldn't hear. 'Be careful, Brody. It's a bad idea to antagonize the Slaydons.'

'I already knew that. But this youngster needs to be taught manners, and I don't think that his father is going to do it.'

'What you saying?' Rick said. 'What you whispering about?' He stepped closer to them.

There had been a few boys hanging around before Rick Slaydon had approached, but now a crowd was gathering. Word had got out that the new blacksmith was trying to commit suicide by making fun of the Slaydon boy.

Tex spoke aloud, so that everybody could hear. 'Now let's not make matters any worse. Brody, why don't you do the work that the boy wants?'

'No, I don't think I will. And not tomorrow either. I don't like his attitude.'

'Not a good idea, Brody.' Tex turned and moved into the doorway and called the apprentice. 'Denny, run and get the sheriff.'

Denny ran off into town, slipping nimbly through the assembled onlookers.

'You're making a mistake, Brody,' Tex said.

'I don't think I am. Can't deal with bullies by placating them.'

'I don't want to lose you on your first day.'

41

'Are you firing me?'

'Nope. But this kid is likely to kill you.'

'Him?' Brody snorted. 'Bigger men have tried.'

Rick Slaydon glared at Brody. 'Want my horse shod.'

Brody just laughed in his face. 'That's not going to happen. Unless you say please.'

Rick's face reddened, and he reached for his gun, clearing it from the holster. Brody threw the blacksmith tongs from his hands, catching the gun and knocking it from Rick's grip. The boy started to scream, as if in pain, although the tongs had only struck the gun, then glared at Brody, and bent down to try to retrieve his weapon.

In an instant, Brody was upon him, grabbing his arm, forcing it behind his back, hard enough to hurt. Brody pushed Rick down on his knees. Then with his free hand, he pushed the boy's face into the dirt.

'Did nobody teach you manners?' Brody asked.

Rick howled.

'Say please,' Brody said.

Rick still howled.

'Say please. I could break your arm very easily, and you wouldn't be able to reach for your gun for weeks.'

Rick screamed, then swore viciously.

'In fact, I could break your arm so badly that you'd never be able to draw a gun again.' Brody pushed Rick's arm harder up his back. 'Say please.'

Rick screamed again, then sobbed, and started shouting. 'Please! Please! Please!'

'That's better,' Brody said, and let the boy's arm loose. Then he kicked him lightly on the rear end, making him sprawl full-length in the dirt. He turned away, scooping up the boy's gun as he did so. 'Since you asked so nicely, Mister Slaydon, I'll have your horse ready for you day after tomorrow.'

Denny returned, accompanied by the sheriff. The crowd parted to let them through.

Tasker said, 'What's going on here?'

Brody said, 'Rick and I had a difference of opinion. I wanted him to say please, and he wanted to shoot me.'

Tasker shook his head. 'Ricky, what are we going to do with you? I thought your pa might have had more sense than to let you back into town so soon.'

Rick got up onto his knees and snivelled. He swore.

'No need for that language, Ricky. You sober?'

'Yessir.'

'Then I'll let you get on your horse and head back to Triple S by yourself. You fit to do that?'

'Yessir.' Rick got up from his knees, and stood, a little shakily.

'I'll have to keep your gun, and I'll take your gun-belt off you as well. You can have them back in a couple of days, if you stay out of trouble.'

Rick grimaced, but said, 'Yessir.'

`Now give me your belt and beat it.'

Rick unfastened his gun-belt and handed it to the sheriff, then walked slowly to his horse, the crowd parting to let him through. He mounted and rode off.

Brody handed Rick's gun to Tasker, who slipped it into its holster.

'I don't think that boy will be the death of me, Brody. But he might be the death of you if you're not careful.'

'I'm always careful, Sheriff. I just don't like bad

manners, or bullies.'

'Neither do I. But when his father's the richest man in the county, we have to put up with things that we don't like.'

'I'm willing to bet that old man Slaydon isn't currently the richest man in the county.'

'How do you make that out?'

'I'm currently in the county. And I'm rich.'

Tasker shook his head. 'You're working in a black-smith's!'

'I work because I like to keep busy. I don't need the money. I've got plenty of my own left to me by my father.'

'You are a strange one, Brody.'

'People have said that to me before.'

'Now that you've crossed both Slaydon and his son, you'll have to watch your back.'

'I always do.'

Brad Stillman came into the sheriff's office the next afternoon at twenty past two and greeted Tasker.

The sheriff replied, 'Good afternoon, Brad. I presume that Dan Slaydon has been talking to you.'

'Indeed, Will. He says he wants to bring charges against the saloon owners for what they did to his boy.'

'And what do you think of that?'

'I think that he's being pig-headed as usual. No judge would take it seriously.'

'I hope you told him that.'

Stillman sighed. 'You know how he is. He thinks that because he's rich, his son can do no wrong.'

'In my experience, Ricky can do no right.'

'You know there's no arguing with the old man.'

'I don't know what you expect me to do, though. I spoke to the people in the saloon. It was one of the customers who threw the boy out, not the bartender or the owner. Nobody was able to tell me who it was. Could have been a stranger who'll be long gone.'

'Slaydon wants to press charges against Bob Rutherford and Louise Delaware.'

'I've got a witness willing to testify that Louise wasn't even there. John Brody, the odd bod who's taken a job at the smithy. In fact, come to that, you're a witness that Louise wasn't there. You were in the stagecoach with her.'

'True.'

'And I'm certainly not going to arrest Bob Rutherford. Old man Slaydon can take it up with me. I don't propose to take the matter any further.'

'Fair enough, Will. I had to come to talk to you about it. I'll tell Slaydon, but he won't like it.'

'Remember to duck when you tell him.'

'I've been dealing with him for a long time. He still makes me nervous.'

The sheriff glanced at the clock on the wall. Half past two. Outside, Brody dismounted from a horse, and stepped into the office.

'Good afternoon, Sheriff. Mr Stillman. I hope you're recovered from our misfortune on the stage yesterday.'

'I'm fine, Mr Brody,' Stillman said. 'I was just discussing some legal matters with the sheriff. I'm just about finished. Perhaps I'll see you later. I'm going to Miss Delaware's theatre tonight to watch her show. She told me she's got some new songs in her act.'

'I might just do that.'

Stillman said, 'She was very taken with you. Said she hoped that you would come and see her perform.'

'Then I will.'

Stillman got to his feet. 'Meanwhile, I've got other work to be attending to. I'll be in my office until six this evening if you need to discuss anything, Will. I'll bid both of you gentlemen a good afternoon.' With that, he left the office.

'How are you, Brody?' Tasker asked. 'Is this business, or a social call?'

'Just a courtesy. I've finished for the day at the smithy, and I've hired a horse from Tex. I'm going to take a ride this afternoon out into the nearby countryside, get the feel of the county. I'm thinking of buying land here-abouts.'

'Settling down here?' Tasker asked.

'Haven't decided yet. I'll ride around, get the lay of the territory. That's why I told Tex I would only work part-time at the smithy, give me time to explore.'

'Be careful if you're going alone. Ricky Slaydon will have spoken to his father about what you did this morning.'

'Youngster had it coming.'

'Maybe so. But his father likes throwing his weight around. You crossed the old man last night when you tried to argue with him. Watch out for trouble.'

'I'll be careful. I just dropped by to tell you what I'm doing, so that you can investigate if I don't come back in the evening.'

'I'll bear that in mind. Mind you take care.'

46

'I always do. See you around, Sheriff.'

'The name's Will.'

'OK, Will. I noticed you've already started calling me Brody, and that will do just fine.'

With that, Brody went out, remounted his horse, and rode away. Tasker watched as Brody headed north, concerned that he might be investigating an 'accident' real soon.

CHAPTER FIVE

The Majestic Theatre took pride of place in the main street, nestled beside the saloon and the Brentwood Falls Hotel. It wasn't quite as imposing as its name suggested, but it was the main source of wholesome entertainment for the town, and impressive by the standards of the territory.

Just before eight o'clock in the evening, Brody stepped out from the entrance of the hotel, and walked the short distance along the boardwalk to the theatre. He had decided to take up Stillman's invitation, especially after the lawyer had hinted that Miss Delaware wanted to see him again.

When he reached the front of the theatre, he stepped back into the street a little way to have a look at it. It was the biggest building in town, slightly larger than the nearby hotel.

Two banners above the doorway proclaimed, '*THE MAJESTIC*' and '*For your delectation, the singing delights of Miss Louise Delaware*'. A poster beside the doorway had a painted portrait of Miss Delaware, full-length, in a scanty, yet somehow still demure, costume. Brody noted that the face was a very good likeness of the woman he had met on the stagecoach.

He entered the theatre. Just inside the door was a small foyer, with a mature lady sitting at a table. Some sort of box-office, Brody surmised.

Brody approached her and said, 'I'd like a ticket to see the show, if I might. Is some payment required here?'

The woman looked up at him and smiled. 'Normally there's a small cover charge. But you're Mr Brody, aren't you?'

'I am.'

'I recognized you from Miss Delaware's description of you. She left instructions that you should be admitted without charge.'

'That's very good of her. There's really no need for that.'

'Miss Delaware insisted. The cover charge is only to deter the more rowdy elements. We make most of our profit selling refreshments.'

'Then I may buy some.'

'Miss Delaware was insistent that you be served refreshment on the house.'

Brody chuckled. 'We'll see about that. Mr Stillman said that he would meet me here. Has he arrived yet?'

'He has.' She picked up a small bell and rang it. A smartly-dressed young man opened the inside door of the theatre and approached.

'Albert,' she said to the young man, 'please show Mr Brody to the table where Mr Stillman is sitting.'

'Yes, ma'am.' Nodding to Brody, Albert added, 'If you

would follow me, sir . . .'

'Lead on, Macduff,' Brody said. Albert shrugged and led the way into the auditorium.

It was unlike theatres Brody knew from back east, although similar to some he had visited in the west, with tables, rather like a large saloon. The tables were of an unusual design, semi-circular, made of walnut, Brody guessed. The straight edges of the table pointed towards the stage, and chairs were set on the rounded sides. Most of the seats were occupied. Albert led Brody to a table near the front of the stage, where Stillman was seated.

The lawyer greeted him. 'Glad you could make it.'

'Wouldn't miss this. Apparently, I'm a special guest of the management.'

'Miss Delaware is impressed by the hero of the hour.'

'I don't know about that. The bandits we faced yesterday. . . . It could have gone very differently if it hadn't been for Curly.'

'Something tells me that you would have found a way,' Stillman said. 'You know everybody in town's talking about you.'

'I guessed there might be some interest in me after the incident at the smithy this morning.' He flushed slightly. 'Does the show start soon?'

'Should be a few minutes. Louise likes the audience to get settled and order their refreshments. She'll pass the word to her pianist to play a short overture when she wants the audience to settle down.'

'One pianist, huh?' Brody said.

'Sometimes there are travelling musicians who are here for a short season. When they come, Louise will employ them, but she puts the cover charge up a bit when she's got a band. There haven't been any, though, for a couple of months.'

'Did the theatre open while she was away?' Brody asked.

'Yes. It usually does. She's got an understudy, a girl she employs as her dresser, who goes on in her place. Good enough girl, sings well enough, but she doesn't draw the audiences the same way.'

Piano music started up. Brody glanced around at the audience. Towards the rear of the hall, Brody spotted the sheriff in deep conversation with a striking young blonde woman. Tasker looked up briefly, noticed Brody, and gave a nod. Brody reciprocated. Looking upwards, he saw that the theatre had box seats. *Very grand for a western town*, he thought. Most boxes weren't occupied, and he guessed that there was a higher cover charge for this luxury seating. He saw that Dan Slaydon and a few other people were sitting in one. Slaydon had observed Brody and was giving him a vicious stare. Brody refrained from acknowledging his presence, certain that the old man would take that as an affront.

The pianist played a fanfare, then began playing a jauntier melody than that of the overture, and after a few bars the curtain opened. Louise Delaware stood in the middle of the stage, beaming a broad smile, and on cue she began to sing.

Brody thought that her voice was too good for a town like this one. She sang a lively number about a lonesome cowboy and his true love. It wasn't a song that Brody knew, but the audience did, and some of them were singing along.

Louise wore a costume that looked identical to the one depicted in the portrait on the wooden banner outside on the theatre's frontage. She sang and carried herself demurely, but the costume was very revealing. It consisted mainly of a tightly-corseted black bodice, with pink lace trim. Brody wondered how she could breathe, never mind sing. Her legs were covered with dark brown silk, sheer to her long, shapely legs. Pink high-heeled shoes completed the ensemble. Brody reckoned she was the finest-looking woman in the county, if not the whole territory.

Her straight brown hair was elegantly coiffured, pinned up in layers to give the impression of her being taller, and not as Brody had seen it on the stagecoach, where it had hung loose under her bonnet. Her stage make-up enhanced her natural beauty, rather than creating a false glamour – which he had sometimes seen in actresses on the stage in Philadelphia and New York. Brody could almost feel the tension amongst the men of the audience, who sat rapt, almost spellbound.

Her first song ended to thunderous applause. With a nod of appreciation to the audience, and Brody could swear that she singled him out with a wink, she then signalled to the pianist who switched to a slower song. The audience, which had been lively during the previous song, now hushed, as if hypnotized by the singer's performance.

Then a third song, another faster melody, this time including a lengthy instrumental break to show off her dancing skills. She danced as well as anybody Brody had seen anywhere, totally confident, knowing instinctively that the steps were perfect for the music. She was no run-of-the-mill saloon singer, but a talent of a higher order.

Before the next number, Louise left the stage for a few moments, then returned, having made a very quick change of costume, into a full-length blue gown. Brody was puzzled by the altered attire, but when he heard the opening bars of the new number, he realized that the singer's garb was appropriate for an operatic aria. Louise sang:

Una voce poco fa
qui nel cor mi risuonò;
il mio cor ferito è già,
e Lindor fu che il piagò.

Brody was astonished. It was Rosina's *Cavatina,* from Rossini's *The Barber of Seville.* He had seen the opera a few years ago, at the Academy of Music in New York, on one of his trips back east. It was the last thing he expected to hear in Arizona. And Louise displayed a fine operatic voice. Brody understood enough music to know she was singing it as Rossini had intended, contralto, in the key of E major. She had been able to switch from pleasing ditties which required an easier vocal style, to this. . . . The audience was transfixed. Brody knew some Italian, so could understand some of the words, but he was sure most of the audience wouldn't know the language at all. However, Louise's vocal abilities had them utterly gripped.

The aria ended, the curtain came down, then came

back up for Louise to acknowledge the applause, and it closed again. The curtain stayed down. The hush which had followed the applause was now broken. Brody wasn't surprised that there was an intermission now – everybody would need some time to get their breath back, not just the performer on stage.

'She's really something, isn't she?' Stillman said.

'I've never seen anything quite like that. Totally surprising and unexpected. And in a town like this . . .'

The sheriff caught Brody's eye, and signalled for him to come over. Brody excused himself to Stillman and strode across to Tasker's table.

'Good evening, Will. I didn't think that this would be your kind of entertainment.'

'Just because I'm an uneducated lawman, doesn't mean I don't appreciate the finer things.'

Brody had no answer to that. He nodded awkwardly to the sheriff's companion.

The sheriff said, 'Where are my manners? Mr John Brody, I'd like you to meet my fiancée. This is Miss Adelaide Summers, our local schoolteacher.'

'Delighted to meet you, Miss Summers,' Brody said.

She offered her hand, and Brody took hold of her fingers lightly, not for a handshake, but as if to raise her hand to his lips to kiss it. But he stopped short of doing that, letting go after a moment.

'You're quite the hero, Mr Brody,' Miss Summers said.

'I don't know about that, ma'am. I just did what I thought was right.'

'I'm glad you stood up to Rick Slaydon. He was a troublesome pupil when I taught him, and he's worse now that he thinks he's grown up.'

'I don't like bullies. He needed to be taught a lesson.'

'What did you think of Louise's performance, Mr Brody?' she asked.

'I'm astonished.'

'My cousin always did have a knack for the unexpected.'

'Your cousin?'

'Why, yes. She came to visit me soon after I got the position as schoolteacher here. She liked the town and decided to stay.'

'Which explains why the local schoolmarm can go to a theatrical entertainment without upsetting her employers. And is able to bring along a crusty old lawman.'

'Now, Mr Brody. Stop teasing.'

'Your servant, ma'am. I should be getting back to my own companion for the evening.'

'Do give my regards to Mr Stillman.'

'I surely will.' He bowed and took his leave, then returned to Stillman.

'An evening of surprises,' Brody said. 'Miss Delaware is the schoolteacher's cousin.'

'Of course she is. I didn't think to mention it.'

The mature lady from the box office approached Brody, coughed, and then said, 'Begging your pardon, sir, but Miss Delaware asked if you would be so kind as to come and meet her in her dressing room.'

'I wouldn't dare to presume.'

'She insists, sir. She said that if I didn't come back with you, she would fire me.'

'In that case, I'll have to comply with her wishes. If

you'll excuse me again, Mr Stillman . . .'

Brody let himself be led to a doorway at the side of the stage, through to the back where there was a door with a prominent pink star, on which the lady knocked.

'Who is it?' came a muffled voice from behind the door.

'Agnes, Miss Delaware. I've brought Mr Brody, like you said.'

'Let him in.'

Agnes pushed the door open to reveal Louise Delaware, standing just inside the door. She was wearing a dressing gown which concealed her body below the shoulders almost entirely. Strangely, Brody found this more alluring than her revealing stage costume.

'Come in, Mr Brody.'

Brody stepped through the doorway.

'That'll be all for just now, Agnes.'

'Ten minutes until the second act, Miss Delaware,' Agnes said.

'I know. I'll be ready.'

She waited until Agnes shut the door.

'Have a seat, Mr Brody. Or may I call you John?'

'I prefer Brody.'

'As a first name?' Louise shrugged. 'I'm Eloisa.'

'But I thought . . .'

'You thought my name was Louise Delaware. On the sign outside it is. It's a stage name. Eloisa Delbrook, at your service . . .' She held out her hand. He took it as he had taken her cousin's a few minutes earlier, but this time he did raise it gently to his lips and kissed it.

'Strictly speaking, it's not Delbrook either. It's my legal

name, but my father came across from Italy as Luigi Del Brucca. It's a family legend that the immigration authorities didn't like it and changed it to Delbrook. I don't know if it's true – Papa was always kidding about things.'

'And Delaware?'

'Like I said, that's a stage name. I didn't think that I could be an actress with the name Eloisa Delbrook. So, I changed it.'

'And so, Miss Delaware sings in a theatre in a small town in Arizona.'

'I suppose I could have changed it again, to Annie Arizona, but that doesn't quite have the same ring to it.' Her laugh was as musical as her singing voice. 'How do you like the show, Brody?'

'*Bellissimo*. I like it fine. Especially the Rossini. Of course, I'm just a humble worker in a blacksmith shop . . .'

Louise tutted. 'Brody, I think we both know that you're far from being that. You're dressed every inch the gentleman, and I think that's exactly what you are.'

'You caught me. I'm an eccentric millionaire, and I shoe horses as a hobby.'

'I don't think you're eccentric. But are you a . . .'

'Millionaire? I suppose so. My father left me a lot of money. I just prefer to work rather than laze about. Manual labour is as good a way of keeping occupied as any. Better than some.'

'I've never met anybody like you, Brody.'

'Nor I you. I didn't think to find somebody so beautiful and talented in . . .'

'. . . A dump like this.'

'I wouldn't have called it a dump.'

'Neither would I. It's a good little theatre, and I'm the top attraction here. Which I wasn't in Philadelphia.'

'You played there?'

'Only in chorus lines. The producers of those shows liked my legs, but they didn't like my voice.'

'Philistines.'

'Exactly. You've heard me sing. But I'd rather be big-time in a hick town than a nobody elsewhere.'

'You wouldn't be a nobody for long.'

'I'm too old for auditions. I like being my own boss.'

'I thought you had a business partner.'

'Bob Rutherford. Yes, but he's not my boss. I run this show. He staked me when I started here. After a couple of years, I bought into his business. He runs the saloon, and the hotel, and we split the profits.'

There was a knock on the door. 'Five minutes, Miss Delaware,' said a male voice from behind the door.

'Thank you, Albert,' Louise called out.

Brody stood up. 'I'd better go and let you get ready.'

'Why don't you wait for me after the show and we can . . . talk some more.'

'I'd like that.' He put his hand out, grasped hers gently, and kissed it again as he had done earlier.

'See you later then, Brody.' She smiled and walked him over to the door. Before opening it, she gave him a peck on the cheek, and then shooed him out.

Brody walked through the backstage corridor and opened the door into the auditorium. He saw that Slaydon had come down from his box and was talking to, or rather arguing with Stillman. The lawyer was frowning as Slaydon waved his fists. The piano music started up again, so that although Stillman was shouting, Brody wasn't able to hear any of Slaydon's raging.

Brody paused in the doorway, knowing that if he went back to sit with Stillman right away, Slaydon's temper would only be worsened. He glanced over at the sheriff, and saw that Tasker was taking a keen interest in the presence of Slaydon at Stillman's table.

After a minute or so, Slaydon clenched his fist, scowled, then shouted once more. Brody still couldn't hear it, but was sure from his lip movements that Slaydon was saying 'This isn't over, Stillman.' Slaydon turned angrily and stomped away.

Brody took his seat at Stillman's table.

'What was all that about?' Brody asked.

'Just business.'

'If Slaydon is annoyed at me sitting with you, I could easily sit somewhere else.'

'Don't worry about it. I've dealt with Slaydon's rages before. What we were discussing has nothing to do with you.' Stillman paused, then said, 'By the way, you've got lipstick on your cheek.'

Brody put his hand to his cheek and rubbed.

'Miss Delaware was just being friendly.'

'She's never been that friendly with me.'

Brody glanced up at the boxes. He could see that Slaydon had returned to his seat and was glaring down at him.

The curtain opened again to reveal Louise, who was dressed in a costume of the same design as before, but now the main colour of her bodice was pink, and the trim was black, as were the shoes. She bowed slightly and began to sing again.

After she had sung a few bars, a loud bang could be heard outside the theatre, followed by a crashing, which went on for about half a minute, rumbling and ominous. Louise had paused, disturbed by the noise. The pianist noted her pause and stopped playing.

'That's odd,' Stillman whispered to Brody. 'No clouds all day. That can't be thunder.'

Louise nodded to the pianist, and he picked up the melody again. She resumed her song, but moments later, the theatre door flew open. Louise stopped again as a man rushed through the doorway. Brody didn't recognize him but could see that he wore a deputy's star. He ran without hesitation to the sheriff's table, knowing exactly where it was without looking. Tasker stood up as he approached.

'What is it, Mikey?' Tasker said.

The deputy said, 'Come quick, Sheriff. Somebody's blown up the jail. Benjy's been hurt, maybe killed.'

CHAPTER SIX

Tasker turned, whispered to Adelaide, and then hurried from the theatre, unaware that all eyes were on him. The deputy, Mikey, followed him out.

Michael Maguire, the younger of Tasker's two regular deputies, slim and rangy, aged thirty, with prominent cheekbones and a square jaw, had a sternness of features which made saloon rowdies think twice about trying to best him in hand-to-hand combat. He had been a deputy for almost five years. Three weeks after taking up the post, he had been nicknamed Mikey by the older deputy, Benjy, and Mikey preferred this to his schoolboy nick-name of Mickey. He had previously had a crush on Miss Summers, but this wasn't reciprocated, and she had made it plain that her romantic interest was solely with the sheriff. Despite this disappointment, Mikey bore no grudge against Tasker, and tried to emulate him, hoping that he could be elected sheriff if ever his boss finally acquiesced to Adelaide's wish that Tasker retire from law enforcement.

As they rushed from the theatre, Tasker asked, 'What happened, Mikey?'

'Benjy had sent me out to do the regular patrol of the town. I'd just finished and was heading back, when there was one almighty bang.'

Tasker could see the plume of smoke rising from the jail and began to run even faster. Mikey struggled to keep up with him, despite being twenty years younger.

Inside the office, Tasker saw dust everywhere, and chairs and cabinets had been blown over. Benjy was on the floor, unconscious and bleeding.

Tasker said, 'Go get Doc Stephens, Mikey.'

Mikey ran out and rode off towards the doctor's house.

Little could be done for Benjy until the doctor arrived. Tasker went to survey the damage to the cells. A large hole had been blown in them. One of the outlaws who'd held up the stagecoach was dead. Tasker glanced at the adjacent cell, saw that this was where the hole in the wall was centred, and that Ishmael was gone.

'Sheriff Tasker?' Brody spoke from the doorway, 'Show's over at the theatre. This was too much of a distraction. A crowd's gathering outside.'

'That's all I need.' Tasker came back along the cell corridor.

'Dynamite?' Brody asked.

'Probably. Big hole in the cell wall. It's made of stone, unlike the rest of the office, to deter prisoners escaping. Didn't work this time.'

'They get away?'

'One of them did. Ishmael. The other one's dead.'

'Maybe we didn't kill as many of the gang as we thought we had.'

'Could be. Some of them might have high-tailed it when they saw that the hold-up wasn't going their way. And there may have been others who didn't take part at all.'

'Possible,' said Brody, pondering. 'That your deputy, Benjy, on the floor there?'

'Yes. He's a good man. . .although if he recovers, don't you dare tell him I said that.'

'Your secret's safe with me. I volunteer as a temporary deputy.'

'I accept the offer.'

'Will you swear me in?'

'OK. You're sworn in. No badge though, and no pay.'

'Don't need any pay. Although I'd take it if it was going. Not bothered about a badge either. I shoot just the same way regardless.'

'I'm going to need volunteers for a posse. We need to try to catch Ishmael and whoever sprung him. They can't have got far yet.'

'Shall I see if I can round up some men?'

'You do that.'

Brody went out to speak to the men in the crowd. Tasker stood in the ruins of his office, not quite sure what to do.

Mikey returned just moments later.

'The doc's on his way. He'll be here in a few minutes.'

'I've deputized Brody. I'm going to have to leave you to guard what remains of this office, while I ride out with a posse to try to catch the people who did this.'

63

Brody returned. 'I've managed to round up ten men.'

The sheriff's firm jaw jutted with determination. 'Go out and tell them to get their horses, and make sure they bring along their handguns. We've also got rifles here that I can issue to some of them.'

'Will do, Sheriff,' Brody said.

The posse rode as hard as the horses would bear, following tracks leading from the jail.

Tasker could see that the trail showed evidence of three horses and a wagon being pulled by two horses, and that they had taken a northwards route. He reckoned it would be light for another hour. He was hopeful that the outlaws could be caught, since they were limited by how fast their horses would go. Tasker's posse had the same limitation, although their horses would be fresher.

Brody rode up beside Tasker.

Tasker said, 'If we can get them before they reach Black Heart Pass, we can catch them. If they make it there, the ground gets rocky and their trail will vanish. Little chance of following them after that.'

'How far is the pass?'

'We can ride fast enough that we can get there in about an hour.'

The sun lowered as the posse rode, darkening the sky, but they were still able to follow the trail. As they reached Black Cactus Hills, the trail veered to the right. It got darker as the sun went below the hill, but they could still see the tracks on the dusty road.

Crack! A sudden shot. One of the horses towards the rear fell, throwing its rider.

The nearest horses tried to bolt. Tasker could see their riders wrestling with the reins. He pulled his mount to a halt and looked around.

'Ambush,' he said. 'Better take cover.'

'Where'd the shot come from?' Brody asked.

'Over in the west, I think, from that hill.'

'I can't see any cover,' said Brody.

'There's a low ridge up ahead.' He turned and shouted to the men following. 'Make for the ridge.'

Sheriff Tasker turned his horse around. 'Brody, I'm going to see to the man who's been thrown.'

He rode back towards the downed rider. It was Carter Sandford, the chandler. He seemed to be unhurt, but his horse was dead.

'You all right, Carter?'

'Just bruised, I reckon.'

'Can you stand?'

'Yep.'

'Jump on my horse, I'll get you to cover.'

Sandford got to his feet and climbed up behind Tasker. They caught up with the posse. A bullet whizzed past Tasker's head, missing him by inches. He drew his gun and returned fire, without much hope of hitting a target.

Reaching the ridge, Tasker considered the options.

'I reckon we've lost our chance of catching the men who blew up the jail,' Tasker said. 'This gunman . . . or men . . . will hold us up here long enough that the rest will get away.' The sheriff looked down at the dirt, and then up again at Brody. 'I suppose it's too much to hope that the shooter would be Ishmael himself. Eh, Brody?'

Brody said, 'One way to find out. We could sneak around behind him.'

'Good idea,' Tasker said. 'You willing to do it, Brody? You go up that way,' he pointed to the left, 'and I'll go up this path over here, and we'll get behind him. The rest of you can distract him by shooting at him.'

Tasker started climbing the hill, and Brody headed up the other path. The trail was tricky, but Brody placed each foot carefully before making the next step. Bits of rock slid underfoot, and he worried about the noise that they made. He was also concerned that there might be more than one gunman. But volleys of gunfire reassured him that however many there were, they would be too occupied to watch for a flank attack.

It was darker now, but Brody knew that he and Tasker could make it before the light was gone. The track began to level as Brody reached a position above the outlaw. It was only a moment before Tasker appeared beside him.

Tasker whispered softly, 'Can you see the guy?'

Brody nodded, not daring to speak.

'Do you think there's more than one?'

Brody shook his head.

'OK, let's do it.' Tasker pulled his gun. Brody was already taking aim.

Tasker spoke loudly. 'Drop the rifle and put your hands in the air.' He flicked the safety on his gun, not having dared to do it earlier.

For a moment, nothing happened. Then the outlaw rolled over and fired his rifle. The slug caught the edge of Brody's coat. Without hesitation, Brody fired.

A sudden cry, and the outlaw dropped his rifle.

Although he had been lying down, Brody's shot had caught him full in the throat. Tasker moved to the spot where the dead outlaw lay sprawled and rolled him over.

'Recognize him?' Tasker asked.

'No.'

'Me neither. I think there aren't any others here; we'd have been attacked right away if there were.'

'Pity he's dead. We still don't know anything about Ishmael, or why he attacked the stagecoach.'

'Had to kill him. He nearly got me. If I'd hesitated, we both could have died.'

'Ishmael has probably got away by now. There's no chance that we'll catch him.'

'I don't think that we've heard the last of him.'

'You're probably right, Brody. Much as I'd like to leave this creature here for the vultures, we have to make sure he gets a burial. Maybe try to find his horse. If we find it, I'm going to give it to Sandford.'

'Shall we drag him down the hill?'

'Yep,' Tasker said. 'We can't possibly make him any uglier than he already is.'

CHAPTER SEVEN

It was after midnight when the posse got back. Weary and downhearted, the men peeled off as they neared their homes. As each left the posse, the sheriff thanked them for their efforts. The last two were Brody and the sheriff. They had found the outlaw's horse on the trail, and Sandford was now riding it. It had a Triple S brand on it, which meant that it was one of Slaydon's horses. Tasker knew that if Slaydon found out about that, he would immediately report that it had been rustled.

As they reached the livery stable, Brody stopped and dismounted. 'Good night, Sheriff,' he said, and started to lead the horse round to the corral at the back. 'I don't want to open up the stable, but I can put my horse in the corral, and attend to it properly in the morning.'

Tasker said, 'I'd better head back, find out what happened to Benjy.'

'I'll check with you in the afternoon, see if you need a hand.'

Brody led his horse around to the corral, as the sheriff turned and rode off into town.

*

Next afternoon, Brody stopped by the sheriff's office.

It had been tidied up, and there was now a dark-brown curtain concealing the corridor to the cells, mainly to prevent a draught from blowing into the office. The blood on the floor had been mopped up.

'Somebody's been hard at work here,' Brody said.

'There wasn't that much damage to the office. We're pretty much back in business, although I've lost two of my three cells until they can be repaired.'

'No arresting bad guys for a while, then.'

'I wish. I've got one cell intact. It'll just be draughty for anybody I have to lock up, until I can arrange for Freddy Anders to repair the wall.'

'I just called by to see if you need me for anything.'

'Everything is under control just now.'

'In that case, I plan to take a ride out to see some more of the countryside.'

'Try to stay away from the Triple S. I'd hate for you to have an "accident".'

'I thought I might ride out along the trail that the outlaws used last night, see what I can see.'

'Be careful.'

'I will.'

Brody rode past the point where the posse had been waylaid the previous day and was following the tracks left by the outlaws. Eventually the dirt trail ended, the terrain got rockier, and the tracks disappeared. The outlaws must have ridden on into the hills. They had a wagon, and that would make the trail more difficult to traverse. It was hard enough for Brody and his horse, so the outlaws would have found it difficult, especially at night. He was sure that they would have to abandon the wagon somewhere.

The land began to dip downhill. It was still rough and rocky, but he carefully picked his way down, coming to level ground. The land to the east flattened out, with a plain stretching out to the horizon, but to the west the hills got higher.

Brody could see, quarter of a mile further on, that there was a cave entrance of sorts at the bottom of the hill. Natural, or man-made? It was difficult to tell from this distance. Perhaps this was what he had been looking for. He rode down to have a closer look.

It was a ruin, but this structure had definitely been carved into the hill by men. There was an abandoned narrow-gauge railroad leading into the entrance. He rode closer, and found a broken hitching post, which would do for tying up his horse.

He stepped into the entrance, and the light cut off abruptly a few yards down the passageway. He reached into his pocket, retrieved a book of matches, and struck one against the rock. It illuminated the mine briefly, long enough for Brody to see that there was a discarded lamp on the floor. The match went out, but Brody was able to feel around for the lamp and set it upright. He carried it out into the light, and saw that it was undamaged, and maybe could still be used. He struck another match, lit the lamp, and carried it into the mine. On the ground a little further in, he saw a wooden board that had fallen off a post. He turned it over. It read: *SLAYDON SILVER. KEEP OUT*. This was what he had been searching for, the reason he had travelled to Brentwood Falls. To keep a promise to his mother. . . .

He walked further into the mine, finding the remains of a fire, which looked fresh, as if it had been extinguished just hours before. This could have been where Ishmael and his gang had stopped for the night. They might have waited through the morning for the return of the man they'd left behind to ambush the posse. Brody wondered how long they had waited before deciding that the man was never coming.

A few more steps into the mine, and Brody shone the lamp around to see if he could learn anything more. He saw something shining in an alcove and went to look at it. It was a fragment of a tin sign, which read: *CARNE SILV*. The lower portion of the sign was covered in dust, but Brody wiped it off, and it read: *Est. 1838*. At least part of what his mother had told him was true. But he had been certain of that since he'd laid eyes on Dan Slaydon in the sheriff's office.

He walked back out of the mine and pondered his next move. Stepping out into the afternoon sunshine, he squinted his eyes with the sudden brightness. When they adjusted, he saw a man standing there.

'Howdy, Mr Brody.'

'Mr Ishmael. I thought you'd be long gone.'

'I thought I would stick around. When I accept a contract from an employer, I try to see it through.'

'Ethical behaviour from an outlaw. Now that's a first.' Brody glanced around, trying to work out if Ishmael was

71

alone. Hard to tell with the cover from the hillside. There was no sign of anybody on the plain, but there was the hill where the mine was situated, and hills on the other side of the valley back along the trail. Members of Ishmael's gang could be hiding. Brody thought ruefully about Tasker's warning on riding out alone.

'Did you wish to speak to me, Ishmael?'

'I reckon that I owe you for what you did to my gang?'

'Gave them what they deserved.'

'Killed half of them.'

Brody shrugged. 'It wasn't just me, though.'

'No, it wasn't. But I'll deal with the others in my own good time.'

'You weren't just robbing the stage, though, were you? There was something else going on, wasn't there?'

Brody was stalling. Ishmael had the drop on him. Brody saw no chance of staying alive if he went for his gun, and there was no cover nearby that he could try to make a dive towards.

Ishmael stood there, gun in hand, not saying anything.

'Well, why did you hold up the stage? There was some other reason, wasn't there?'

'Maybe there was, maybe there wasn't.'

'You might as well tell me. Seeing as you're going to kill me anyway, what difference does it make?'

'It makes a difference to me, Brody.'

'You going to kill me?'

'Why don't you reach for your gun? Then we'll see.'

Brody pondered. 'No, I don't think that I will. It wouldn't do me any good.'

'Makes no difference to me. All I've got to do is

squeeze this trigger.'

'Will that please old man Slaydon?'

Brody saw Ishmael's eyes widen at the mention of Slaydon.

'Who?' Ishmael said. 'Who's this Slayton? Never heard of him.'

'You know exactly who Slaydon is. He paid you to hold up the stagecoach and busted you out of jail.'

'Nobody named Slayman busted me out.'

'He wasn't there in person, I know that. I saw him with my own eyes, in the theatre. He was there watching Miss Delaware perform.'

'That bitch. After I've dealt with you, she'll get hers.'

Brody's fists tightened. He must have reddened in the face too, showing some anger, because there was a change in Ishmael's demeanour. He had been finding the situation amusing, but now there was a coldness in his face.

He thumbed the safety on his revolver and took aim at Brody.

There was a sudden gunshot.

Brody winced, then realized he hadn't been hit. He also saw bafflement in Ishmael's face. The shot hadn't been from Ishmael's gun, nor was it aimed at Brody. There was another shot, which kicked up dust in front of Ishmael.

Brody took advantage of the hesitancy of Ishmael's reaction, and dived to the ground, rolling over so that he could draw his revolver before he faced towards Ishmael again. Ishmael started shooting, but his aim was off. Brody fired. He too missed, with the bullet whizzing over

Ishmael's head.

Brody saw that Ishmael was cursing his luck. The outlaw looked around, trying to see where the shots were coming from. He ran behind a rock outcrop just yards from the mine entrance.

Brody heard footsteps behind him, and swiftly turned around, ready to take aim.

'Brody?' It was Tasker. 'Are you all right?'

'Sheriff! Shouldn't creep up on a man. I might have shot you. What are you doing here?'

'I'm following you,' he said. 'I didn't think that it was a good idea for you to go riding on your own, so I followed you.'

'That really wasn't necessary. I can look after myself.'

'You were doing a real good job of it, I can see. When I caught up to you, Ishmael had the drop on you, so I started shooting at him.'

'Pity you missed. Although I think I know who his boss is.'

'Who?'

'Slaydon. Good old Dan "Triple S" Slaydon.'

'Ishmael told you this?'

'No. But he reacted when I said it. I'm sure that Slaydon paid Ishmael to hold up the stagecoach. And organized the jail-break.'

'Why would he do that? I've no liking for Slaydon, but he's no outlaw. And there's no evidence against him.' Tasker looked around. 'I don't think that there's any point in trying to go after Ishmael now. He'll be well gone.'

'We also don't know if any of his gang are waiting for

him.' Brody shook his head. 'The two of us wouldn't stand a chance against a gang of them.'

'Let's go back to town,' Tasker said. 'I hope you'll heed my advice now about riding in this countryside alone.'

'I will. Anyway, I think I've found what I was looking for.'

'And what's that?'

'I'd rather not say just now. I'll tell you when and if you need to know.'

Brody unhitched his horse, and the two men walked back along the trail to Tasker's horse. Then they rode back to town in silence.

CHAPTER EIGHT

Brody went to the hotel to freshen up before dinner. As he went to walk up the stairs to his room, the desk clerk called to him.

'Mr Brody, there's a letter for you.'

He held out the envelope, and Brody took it, noting that it was lavender-coloured, and had a faint feminine perfume. He slipped it into his coat pocket and went to his room. Once there, he ripped open the envelope. The letter inside was a note from Louise Delaware. It read:

Dear Mr Brody,

My cousin Adelaide Summers and I would be delighted if you would join us for Sunday lunch at our house. I still haven't been able to thank you properly for the way you protected me from the outlaws who held up the stagecoach. We would be pleased if you would join us on Sunday afternoon after church.

Please say that you will join us. It will only be a small gathering. Sheriff Tasker, Adelaide's fiancé, usually joins us, so it would be the four of us.

Your most humble admirer,

Eloisa Del Brucca.

Brody felt this was an honour she didn't give out lightly, and he preferred to have Sunday lunch in company, rather than by himself in the hotel. He went to the writing desk, swiftly and neatly drafted a reply accepting the invitation, folded the letter, and placed it in an envelope. He decided that he would take it to the theatre himself and stay to watch the show.

Stillman was working late in his office. He finished off what he was doing, slid the papers into a drawer, and locked it. He stood up, reaching for the coat-hook on the wall, so that he could put on his coat. There was a sudden creak of the floorboards behind him. He looked around. Nobody there.

He stepped around the desk and put on his coat. Another creak. He began to feel a deep dread that some phantom had come to haunt him. He knew it was superstitious nonsense but shivered nonetheless. Just hunger affecting his mood, he thought. Once he had a good supper, he would be restored to his normal equanimity.

Another floorboard creaked, nearer this time.

'Who's there?' he called out.

'Who do you think?' a voice answered.

'If I knew, I wouldn't be asking.' He looked around again. Still nobody there. 'Is that you, Slaydon?'

A guttural laugh came from behind him.

'And why would Slaydon be coming to see you at this time of night?' the voice asked. 'And wouldn't he come in the front door instead of sneaking around in back.'

'I suppose so,' the lawyer said.

'You know so.'

Stillman was sure that he had heard the voice before, but couldn't place it. 'Do I know you? Did I defend you? Or prosecute you?'

'We've never met in a professional capacity. *Your* professional capacity, that is. But we have met in *my* professional capacity.'

'And what is your profession, sir?'

'Outlaw.'

Stillman wanted to run, but fear froze him to the spot. A rope went around his neck and tightened. Then tightened yet further. He struggled for breath. His hands reached to his neck, frantically pulling at the cord that was choking him, to no avail. The rope was being pulled by strong and determined hands.

'Time to die, Stillman.'

Stillman tried to resist, pulling, pushing, kicking his legs backwards in the vain hope of contact with his assailant. One last mighty heave, and he managed to turn around to see the face of his killer.

The outlaw cackled.

'Call me Ishmael,' he said, and pulled yet tighter, choking the final breath out of Stillman.

Tasker knocked on the door of Benjy's house. He waited a moment and heard the bolt on the door being snapped back.

The door opened, and Benjy's wife stood there, pleased to see the sheriff.

'Good evening, Ella. I hope that Benjamin might be up to greeting a visitor.'

'Will, good to see you,' Ella said. 'Benjamin is lying down, because the doctor told him to take it easy, but I'm quite sure that he wouldn't want me to turn you away.'

'Who is it, Ella?' came a muffled voice from inside the house.

'It's Will Tasker,' Mrs Britton called out.

'That you, boss? Come in and warm your boots by the fire.'

It was July, and there was no fire.

Ella stood aside to allow the sheriff to enter. Benjy was lying on a cot near the unlit fire, and there was a chair nearby, upon which Tasker sat.

'I thought you were a goner, Benjy.'

'No sirree. Take more than that to put Benjy out of action. Only thing I'm sorry about is that they got the jump on me.'

'Do you remember what happened?' the sheriff asked.

'It was about an hour after you'd gone across to the theatre with Miss Adelaide, to see Miss Delaware's show. Somebody came into the office, pulled a gun on me. His mouth was covered, so I only saw his eyes. He thrust his gun in my belly, told me to shut up. So, I did. He called out to Mr Ishmael to get as close as he could to the cell door, and to crouch down. Didn't say anything to the other prisoner, who was asleep in any case. Then there was one almighty noise, and rubble and dust and smoke everywhere. Must have been a big hole in the cell wall, I reckon. That right, boss?'

Tasker nodded.

'I tried to make a move, and the fella shot me. Because I moved, he didn't get me in the belly. I'da been a goner if he did.'

Tasker said nothing.

'Did you catch them?' Benjy asked.

'No,' Tasker admitted.

'I reckon I'll need to be up on my feet and back to work as soon as I can. You're just no good without me.'

Tasker chuckled.

There was an urgent pounding at the door.

'Who can that be?' Ella asked.

The banging at the door kept on.

'Hold on, hold on,' Ella said. 'What's got into people tonight? Never get a visitor from one week's end to the next, now there are two in five minutes.'

She opened the door, and Mikey rushed in. 'Begging your pardon, ma'am. Sorry to interrupt, Sheriff, but you're needed at the whorehouse. Begging your pardon again, ma'am, for the language.'

Ella smiled faintly.

The sheriff said, 'And just what is it that requires my attention at the . . . house of ill repute.'

'One of the wh . . . er, ladies . . . has been murdered.'

'They catch who did it?'

'Yes, boss.'

'Well . . . who did it?'

'It was Rick Slaydon.'

'Damn. Begging your pardon, ma'am.'

Ella said, 'Quite all right, Will. I'd curse too if I had to arrest that Slaydon boy.'

'I'd better go and do that. I'll call again for a more sociable visit tomorrow, if I can.' He tipped his hat and went out.

Tasker saw that there was a light in the lawyer's office. 'Mikey, you'd better run over to Stillman's office, tell him the Slaydons will be needing his professional services.'

'Sure thing, boss.' Mikey set off towards the lawyer's office.

La Maison De L'Amour was set half a mile outside of town, because the more religious townspeople considered the whole business immoral. It was far enough away that Tasker rode to it rather than walk.

The sheriff visited the place now and then, not as a customer, but because he liked to stay friendly with everybody in town. He liked Yvette Lamoureux, the madam, who was really a no-nonsense Texan named Beulah Johnson. Tasker always addressed the madam by her real name, and she liked him well enough to allow it, although she would never permit such a liberty from anybody else.

As the sheriff arrived, the madam herself was standing in the open doorway, and waved to him at his approach.

'Good evening, Beulah,' he said. 'I hear you've had some trouble.'

'Bad business, Will. I should have turned that Slaydon boy away. But he's never been as bad as this before.'

'What did he do?'

'He came in here, drunk. Demanded a session with

81

Genevieve.'

Tasker knew that following the style of the house, all the girls had French names, despite none of them being French.

Yvette continued, 'I let Genevieve take him upstairs. Seemed all right at first, but then the screaming started.'

Yvette led Tasker into the parlour where various girls were sitting, stunned. Some of them were weeping and all had ashen complexions.

'I ran upstairs with Brandon,' Yvette said. Tasker knew Brandon Smith, Beulah's black man-servant, the only male in a house full of women. Good to have a big man around, give the customers second thoughts about causing trouble. 'Brandon burst open the door, which was locked. I always tell the girls not to lock their doors, but sometimes the customers pay them extra to do it. Genevieve was on the bed, and her throat was cut. Rick Slaydon was just sitting on the *chaise longue*, holding a blood-stained knife, bawling his eyes out.'

'Where is he now?'

'Brandon has him restrained in the back room.'

'I'll see to that later. Can I have a look at the scene of the crime?'

'Sure. Doc Stephens is up there. I sent Minette to get him, in case there was anything that could be done for Genevieve.'

'I'll go there now, if I may.'

Yvette led Tasker to the rooms on the second floor. Genevieve's room was the second on the left along the hallway, and the door was ajar. Doc Stephens was there, washing his hands at a sink.

'Hi, Doc,' the sheriff said. 'Anything that can be done for the girl?'

'Afraid not, Will,' Doc Stephens said. 'The main artery was opened. She'd have bled to death within seconds.'

Tasker glanced at the figure on the bed, covered in blood, staring the grim stare of the dead.

'I take it that there's no doubt about what happened here.'

'None,' Yvette said. 'Brandon and I both saw Rick with the knife in his hand.'

'I'll have to arrest him then. You'd better take me to him.'

Yvette led Tasker down to the public parlour and along a corridor to her private room where Rick was being restrained in handcuffs. Tasker knew, because Beulah had told him, that she had a few sets of handcuffs on the premises, because some of the customers liked them as part of the service. Tasker wasn't acquainted with that kind of thing, more used to using them on prisoners.

'Ricky, what are we going to do with you?'

'Want my pa.'

'Really, Ricky? The last time, you didn't want him. You really should make up your mind.'

'Want my pa.'

'Later. I'd like to talk to you first.' The sheriff moved nearer to the table, but didn't sit down. 'Why did you kill Genevieve?'

'Didn't.'

'Now, Ricky. There are two witnesses say you did.'

'Didn't. Want my pa.'

83

'You have to tell the truth if we're going to help you. Why did you kill Genevieve?'

'Didn't.'

'Then who did?' Tasker asked.

'Man.'

'What man?'

'Man hiding in closet.'

Tasker shook his head. The boy was a simpleton.

'What man?' the sheriff repeated.

'Man hiding in closet.' Rick was a boy of few words, often repeated.

'Do you know this man, Ricky?'

'Uh-hnn.' That was the best that Rick could muster when he meant 'no'.

'Ever see him before?'

'Uh-hnn.'

Questioning Rick was a waste of time. He turned to Yvette and Brandon.

'Did either of you see anybody else in Genevieve's room?'

'No, sir,' Brandon said.

'Nobody else there,' Yvette said.

That appeared to settle it.

'What did this man do?' Tasker asked Ricky again.

'Cut Genevieve's throat. Threatened to cut my throat too, if I didn't stop screaming.'

'What did you do?'

'Stopped screaming.'

'What happened then?'

'Man put knife in my hand, went away.'

'And where did he go?'

'Back in the closet.'

'Why didn't you shoot him?' Tasker asked.

Rick's mouth gaped open. 'Didn't think of it,' he said.

'This is ridiculous.' Tasker sighed in exasperation. He turned away from Rick.

'Beulah. Brandon. Could what the boy is saying be true? Could there have been some strange man in Genevieve's closet?'

'Don't see how,' Brandon said. 'I open the door to most of the customers. They're all accounted for. Those who weren't down in the main parlour before going upstairs were already upstairs in a room with one of the girls.'

'How many were there?'

'Seven,' Yvette said. 'All accounted for. I make them pay up-front, so that they don't get funny after they've finished. I enter it up in a book. I give all the customers code-names. No strangers in the house tonight.'

'I'll need to know who was here,' Tasker said.

'Will, I guarantee our customers total discretion.'

'I know that. I don't care who they are or why they were here. Are any of them still here, by the way?'

Yvette shook her head. 'They all left. Couldn't wait to get out of here.'

'I'll bet. I'll need to speak to them. I can be discreet too. I don't want to disrupt your business any more than you want to disrupt mine.'

'I'll make a list for you, Will.'

'Thanks, Beulah.' Tasker turned again to the Slaydon boy. 'Now, Ricky, I'm going to have to take you in.'

'What for?' Rick asked.

'You know what for. You're going to have to come to jail to await trial for the murder of Genevieve.'

'Didn't.'

'Madame Lamoureux and Mr Smith here say that you did.'

Rick scoffed. 'A whore and a ni . . .'

Tasker cuffed Brandon's cheek with the back of his hand. 'You'll keep a civil tongue in your head, young man.'

Rick snivelled. 'Want my pa.'

'We'll see about that later.' Tasker manoeuvred the boy to his feet, led him towards the door. Turning to Yvette, he said, 'I'd be obliged, Beulah, if I could borrow your handcuffs, seeing as the boy's already got them on. I'll see that they're returned to you in the morning.'

Yvette went to a cupboard, opened it, took out a key and offered it to Tasker. He waved it away, saying, 'No need for that. All cuffs of the same manufacture have the same lock. The jail's keys will open these.'

Tasker got his prisoner to his feet, and led him out, with Yvette following them. As they got to the main parlour, Tasker heard a fierce pounding coming from the outer door. Tasker saw that Doc Stephens was still there, issuing sedatives to the distressed girls. One of the girls opened the door. Standing in the doorway was Mikey, the deputy.

'Sheriff, you gotta come. Stillman's been murdered.'

'Wasn't me,' Rick said.

'Shut up, Ricky,' Tasker said. 'We know that one wasn't you. Stop annoying me.'

'Want my pa,' Rick said.

'That will have to wait,' Tasker said.

'Want my pa,' Rick said.

'Not now, Ricky,' Tasker said.

CHAPTER NINE

After they left the whorehouse, Tasker asked Mikey what had happened.

'I went to Mr Stillman's office, just like you told me to. There was a light on, so I reckoned he hadn't finished for the day. I knocked on the door, but there was no answer.'

'Then what?' Tasker asked.

'Pushed the door, and it opened. I went in, and there was Mr Stillman, slumped on his desk. Dead. A rope around his neck.'

Tasker swore softly. 'Mikey, you'd better take Ricky to the jail, lock him up. I'll go to Stillman's office.'

Doc Stephens had just caught up with them, and said, 'I suppose I had better come too, Will.'

'You can confirm that he's dead, at least.'

Mikey led Rick Slaydon away. Doc had his wagon, so Tasker hitched his horse to the back of it, and they drove to Stillman's office. When they got there, the doctor hurried over to Stillman, and felt for a pulse.

'He's dead all right.' Doc Stephens lifted Stillman's head and examined the rope around his neck. The dead hands were still clutching it. Eyes bulging. Doc loosened the rope a little and looked more closely.

'Strangled. Lacerations around the neck.'

Tasker's eyes darted around the office. 'Assailant must have sneaked up behind him. He probably didn't even know who it was. Might not even have heard him.'

'Maybe,' the doctor said.

'There's no real sign of any disturbance. Papers knocked to the floor, but that could have happened in the struggle. And no sign that the office has been searched for anything. What time of death would you estimate?'

The doctor touched the back of the corpse's right hand.

'*Rigor mortis* hasn't set in. That would take at least two hours. Sometimes twice that or possibly more. Temperature's not dropped that much. This can't have happened any more than an hour ago.'

'Which means that the perpetrator can't have got far. I'll have to examine the scene, then find out if there were any witnesses.'

'Anything you need from me, Will?' the doctor asked.

'Would you go to my office and tell Mikey to come?'

The doctor nodded and left. Tasker did a quick survey of the scene. Little had been disturbed. He examined the floor behind the lawyer's chair, and saw that there were footmarks, but they had been stepped over several times.

A short time later, Mikey arrived.

'I've got Rick Slaydon locked up, boss.'

'That's good. I want you to guard this office just now, make sure nobody comes in without my say-so.'

'OK, boss.'

Tasker exited the office. He had no expectation of there being any evidence at the front of the office, either on the boardwalk or the street, because he was sure that the attacker had approached from the back. So he slipped through the little lane at the side of the premises, to the rear of the building. A quick examination showed one set of footprints, and hoofmarks. Clearly the attacker had come by horse, so would be long gone. The neighbouring buildings had no windows at the back. Later, he would ask the shop proprietors whether they had seen anything, but he held out little hope.

Tasker thought that it might be better to go through Stillman's files to see if there was information suggesting any enemies that Stillman might have had. He would need a lawyer to go through Stillman's papers for him. But Stillman had been the only lawyer in town, and the nearest one would be in Silver Springs. Then it occurred to him. Of course, there was another lawyer in town. Brody. He had said that he had never practised law, but he would understand these papers all right. 'Deputy' Brody would do it, Tasker was certain.

He went back inside Stillman's office and told Mikey to go and get the undertaker. 'Tell him that he's got two bodies, one here and one at the brothel. Tell him to come here first.' He spotted the key to the office in a tray on the desk in front of Stillman's corpse. 'We'll lock up here just now, and you can take the key so that you can let the undertaker in. I'm going to see if I can find Brody.'

As they left, Tasker locked the office, and gave the key

to Mikey. Tasker then headed towards the hotel, and Mikey went in search of Raleigh the undertaker.

When Tasker asked for Brody, the desk clerk informed him that Brody had gone to the theatre. On enquiring at the Majestic, Tasker smiled wryly when Agnes informed him that Brody was visiting Miss Delaware in her dressing room during the interval. He told Agnes that he needed to see Brody on official business, and she took him backstage.

Agnes knocked when they got to the dressing room door. 'Miss Delaware. The sheriff is here, wants to speak to Mr Brody.'

After a moment, Louise opened the door. 'Thank you, Agnes. Come in, Will.'

The sheriff entered, and saw Brody sitting on the *chaise* which Louise used for entertaining her guests.

'I'm here on business, I'm afraid,' Tasker said. 'Mr Stillman has been killed.'

Louise gasped. 'No!'

'I don't believe it,' Brody said.

'I've just come from his office. He's been strangled.'

'Poor man,' Louise said.

'Any idea who did it?' Brody asked.

'Nope.'

'I take it that there's some reason you wanted to speak to me,' Brody said.

'Yep. Stillman was the only lawyer in town. The nearest one is in Silver Springs, and you know how far away that is. I thought that his legal papers might shed some light on who killed him . . .'

'And that I might be able to help you with that.'

'You told me a couple of days ago that you were a qualified lawyer.'

'Really?' Louise said. 'You never told me that. You are a surprising man, Brody.'

'I don't like to boast.'

Tasker said, 'I thought that maybe you could go through Stillman's papers.'

'I could do it tomorrow afternoon.'

'That'll be fine, Brody. Call on me then, and I'll let you have the key to Stillman's office.'

There was a knock at the door. 'Five minutes, Miss Delaware.'

'I'll be ready, Albert,' Louise called to the door. 'Now if you gentleman would excuse me . . .'

'Lou,' the sheriff said, tipping his hat.

'I'll come backstage again after the show,' Brody said. 'I can walk you home.'

'I'd like that.'

The two men took their leave. As Sheriff Tasker closed the door, he motioned to Brody.

'There's something else that I didn't want to mention in front of Miss Delaware. Stillman wasn't the only person murdered tonight. One of the girls in the brothel was killed.'

'By a customer?'

'Yes. Rick Slaydon. I've got him locked up, but that might be even more trouble. Once old man Slaydon finds out . . .'

'Rather you than me.'

'I think,' Tasker said, 'that Slaydon hates you more than he hates me. But it's a close-run thing.'

'Well, you're probably right at that, Sheriff.'

'Call me Will.'

'I'm still deputized?'

'You are,' confirmed the sheriff.

'Then it's "boss" or "sheriff", unless it's a social call.'

'Fair enough, Brody,' Tasker said. 'What are you going to do now?'

'I'm going back into the theatre to see the rest of the show. I never got to see the end of it last time, because of the jail break.'

'You said that you'd be walking Lou home after the show.'

'That's right.'

'When you get there, would you give Miss Summers a message for me?'

'Happy to oblige.'

'Tell her about what's happened tonight. Certainly, about Stillman, I'll leave it to your discretion about the other matter. You can tell her that I'll be too busy to see her tomorrow, but that I'll certainly see her for lunch on Sunday.'

'I'll be there too,' Brody said. 'Louise invited me . . .'

As he turned to leave, Tasker said, half to himself, 'Why am I not surprised?'

Around nine-thirty the next morning, Tasker's office door was thrown open violently, and Dan Slaydon barged in. He loomed in front of the sheriff, face like thunder.

'What can I do for you this morning, Mr Slaydon?' the sheriff asked.

'I've come for my boy.'

'To do what?'

'Are you deliberately trying to be obtuse, you miserable little man?'

Tasker stood up from his chair, showing his full height. 'I'd thank you, Mr Slaydon, not to insult me.'

'You miserable pipsqueak. I could break you in half.'

'Six bullets in this gun say you couldn't.' Tasker gently rested a finger on the butt of his gun but made no attempt to remove it from the holster.

'You wouldn't dare.'

'Don't push me, Mr Slaydon.'

'Give me my boy.'

'No. He's been arrested for murder. I have to keep him incarcerated until he stands trial.'

'I'll be getting my lawyer to speak to you about this. When I can find him. Where is that idiot, Stillman? He wasn't in his office when I went there.'

'You'll find him at the undertaker.'

'The undertaker? What in blazes is he doing there?'

'Occupying a coffin.'

'Occupying a. . . .' Slaydon's brow furrowed, then the sheriff's meaning occurred to him. 'You mean he's dead?'

'As dead as that prostitute your boy murdered.'

'I don't think that you can compare a respectable lawyer to a cheap whore.'

The sheriff snorted. 'From what Madame Lamoureux tells me, all her whores are pretty expensive. You would know that better than me.'

'How dare you! Give me my boy right now.'

'No.'

'Tasker, do you have some sort of death wish? Give me my boy right now, or you'll be in big trouble.'

'I can't do that. He murdered a human being and has to stand trial.'

'The world has been rid of a worthless whore.'

'Is that you, Pa?' Rick Slaydon had woken up.

Slaydon stepped to the curtain and tore it down. Tasker walked forward, in case he had to intervene, and saw that Slaydon was waving his fist at the cell.

'You worthless piece of crap, Rick. What did you have to go and kill a whore for?'

Rick blubbered. 'Didn't, Pa.'

'Didn't? What do you mean, didn't?'

'Man did it.'

'What man?'

'Don't know. Came out the closet, slit Genevieve's throat, threatened to do the same to me.'

'Did you tell the sheriff this?'

'Yes, Pa. He didn't believe me.'

'We'll see about that.' Slaydon turned to Tasker. 'Tasker, you heard the boy. He didn't do it. Let him go right now.'

'Can't do that,' the sheriff said. 'There's no evidence of this man. Rick had the knife in his hand, and he was alone with the victim. He has to stand trial.'

'Tasker, be reasonable. You let my boy go right now, or you're finished in this town.'

'Can't do that, Slaydon. I suggest that you leave this office right now.'

Slaydon clenched his fists, almost turning purple with rage.

'You haven't heard the last of this, Tasker.'

Slaydon barged out of the cell corridor, bumping Tasker on the shoulder as he went past, then stormed out of the office.

No, thought Tasker, *I don't suppose I have.*

CHAPTER TEN

Walking back from church on Sunday morning, Louise and Adelaide took the arms of Brody and Tasker respectively. Tasker whispered to Adelaide, and then spoke aloud.

'I have to go and check in on Mikey before I join you for lunch. It won't take long. Perhaps you would come with me, Brody?'

Brody hesitated. 'Don't the ladies need to be accompanied?'

Adelaide said, 'Mr Brody, we're not exactly helpless.'

'Go ahead, Brody,' Louise said. 'It will give us time to get the lunch ready.'

'Well, in that case . . .'

Adelaide kissed Tasker on the cheek, and Louise did the same to Brody. Then they set off towards their house.

As the men continued down the street, Tasker asked, 'How are you getting on with Stillman's papers?'

'Most everything seems in order. Just the usual things you would expect.'

'Pity,' the sheriff said.

'Except ... I found absolutely no mention of Dan Slaydon. From what I understood, Stillman was his lawyer.'

'You're absolutely right. Far as I know, all Slaydon's legal business in Perth County was handled by Stillman.'

'Then the files should be there. But there was nothing. I could understand it if Stillman was doing some shady deals for Slaydon, the papers for those would be hidden. But some work would be legitimate, and there's no sign of any at all. Did you search Stillman's house?'

'I did. Mikey helped me. No legal papers at all.'

In Tasker's office, there was a surprise visitor.

'Benjy!' Tasker said. 'How are you feeling? Are you sure you should be here?'

'That's what my wife said to me. But I was getting under her feet at home. So, I thought I would come see you. I walked all the way here, and it didn't hurt ... much. I'd like to come back to work, just minding the office, and what's passing for a jail now that it's been blown up.'

'If the doc agrees, I'll let you come back to work.'

Then Tasker turned to Mikey. 'Anything else I should be aware of?'

'Don't think so, boss.'

'No trouble from our prisoner?'

'Apart from wanting his pa.'

'And what about his pa?' Tasker asked.

'Haven't seen any sign of him. You expecting trouble?'

'Maybe. Pity we haven't got more deputies. Slaydon's liable to do anything.'

'I'm still deputized,' Brody said.

'We'll probably need you,' Tasker said. 'I suggest we take a stroll to the ladies' house and join them for lunch.'

'Good idea,' Brody said.

It was a ten-minute walk to the women's cottage on the outskirts of town. As they approached, Brody felt a sudden unease, and drew his gun.

'Something doesn't feel right,' he said.

Tasker nodded, and his hand went instinctively to the gun holstered on his left hip. He broke into a run, and Brody started to follow, overtaking easily. As they neared, he saw that the reflection of the sun on the window was distorted where the pane had been broken, and the door was lying open. They rushed in to find that the women weren't there. One of Adelaide's shoes lay forlornly on the floor.

Tasker looked into the other rooms. 'Nobody here.'

Brody paced around, trying to get a sense of what had happened.

'The stove is warm,' he said. 'In fact, it's on.' Brody opened its door and saw that roast beef was cooking. Brody glanced at the meat and could see that it had recently been turned over in its pan.

Tasker said, 'Addie and Lou must have got back here. Somebody has interrupted them . . .'

'. . . and taken them,' finished Brody. 'But who would do that?'

'Slaydon, maybe?'

'Surely not.'

Tasker shook his head. 'He's always been hot-headed. But Stillman was mostly able to stop him from doing anything too crazy. With Stillman dead, Slaydon is capable of just about anything. I've only known him for ten years, but the old-timers remember him from way back. He was a no-good, arrogant youngster, hopeless as a cow-puncher, a bit better as a silver miner.'

'He wouldn't have kidnapped Louise and Adelaide, would he?'

'It's possible. Everybody in town knows of my engagement to Addie, and he'll be aware that something's going on between you and Lou . . .'

Brody stood, pondering.

'Sheriff, there's something I should tell you.'

'What? That you're Slaydon's long-lost son?'

'No. But I think that I'm the rightful owner of Slaydon's silver mine.'

'That lode was played out years ago,' the sheriff said. 'Slaydon took the money and bought a ranch, then Triple S, named after himself, his brother and his son.'

'But the silver mine wasn't his to begin with, was it?'

'No. It belonged to Henry Carne.'

'And when he died, it should have passed to his daughter. Jemima Carne. My mother.'

'Your mother? Does Slaydon know that?'

'I don't think so. I never told anybody my real name.'

'You aren't John Brody?'

'That was my father. *My* name is Carne Brody.'

'So, it isn't coincidence that you've come to Brentwood Falls?'

'No. My mother told me about Slaydon, and how he took advantage of her . . .'

'Improper advances, you mean?'

'No, he wouldn't have dared. But he *had* worked his way up to become Henry Carne's foreman. When my grandfather died, a will was discovered, leaving the mine to Slaydon. I didn't know anything about this until a few weeks ago. When my mother was dying, she sent for me, and told me the whole story. She made me pledge that I would come to Brentwood Falls and right the injustice that was done to her.'

'So that's why you've come here.'

'Everything else I've told you is completely true. My father was a very rich man, and now that my mother's dead, I've inherited everything.'

'If Slaydon suspects your real identity, that could give him reason to abduct Lou.'

'I doubt that he does. In any case, I've already made an enemy of him.'

'You sure have.' The sheriff chuckled mirthlessly.

'What do we do now?' Brody asked.

'First of all, I'm going to check around the grounds of this house. Look for tracks. I know Addie and Lou would have put up a fight. There's bound to be some sign of that.'

They found nothing out front, but there were definite signs of struggle behind the house. Various footprints and hoof marks, and the wheels of a wagon. Some footprints were of a bare foot, which had to be Adelaide. The tracks led south, in the direction of the Triple S ranch.

Brody rubbed his hands together nervously. 'Shouldn't we raise a posse, go after them? They can't be that far ahead of us.'

'No point. I think we'll get a message from the kidnappers real soon. Then we'll know what action to
take.'

Brody was unconvinced, but there would be no point
in him trying to pursue the kidnappers by himself.

Tasker went back into the house and turned off the
stove. 'No point in letting the house burn down,' he
said.

Then they trudged back into town. Brody suddenly felt
very weary.

They didn't have long to wait.

A blond-haired boy aged about ten ran breathlessly
into the sheriff's office and halted in front of his desk.

'Sheriff,' he said. 'A man asked me to give you a note.'
He held out an envelope.

'What man?' the sheriff asked.

'Just a man. Never seen him before. I was playing
outside the livery stable, and he came up to me. Asked
me to give you a note. Said you would give me a dime.'

'Cheapskate,' remarked Brody. 'Couldn't even pay for
it himself. Still, I suppose that made sure you would
deliver it.'

'What's your name, boy?' Tasker asked.

'Billy.'

'Billy what?'

'Billy Sullivan.'

'Does your mom know that you're out?'

'Yessir, she always lets me go down to the livery stable
on Sunday afternoons. I like it a lot better than church.
School, too.'

102

'I suppose you would at that. Can you describe this man?'

'Big man with a black hat.'

'What about his face?'

'It was a man's face.'

'All the men in the world have a man's face,' said Brody. 'That really narrows it down.'

'Anybody else see him, Billy?' Tasker asked.

'Don't think so.'

Billy held out the envelope to Tasker, and also his other hand in expectation of payment before he handed it over. Brody fished a dime out of his pocket and gave it to the boy, who then let the envelope fall onto the sheriff's desk.

Tasker picked it up. 'Run along now, Billy. And if you see that man again, come and tell me.'

'Sure thing, Sheriff.' Billy ran out without a further word.

Tasker tore the envelope open, examined the note within and read it quickly. Then he handed it to Brody who read the letter aloud.

'Good afternoon, Sheriff Tasker.

'We have taken Miss Summers and Miss Delaware. They are unharmed . . . presently.'

Brody looked at Tasker. 'Presently. I don't like the sound of that.'

'Neither do I,' Tasker said. 'Go on.'

Brody continued: 'We are willing to trade them for Richard Slaydon. If you bring him to the Falls, we can make the exchange there. There should be no attempt at bringing a posse. If there is, the ladies will be killed. The only person we will allow to accompany you and your prisoner, is Mr Brody. In fact, we insist that Mr Brody be present.

'If you comply with our request, there should be no further unpleasantness.

'Tomorrow at three o'clock is when we will make the exchange. We advise that you arrive no earlier than that, or we will not answer for the consequences.

'Signed, A Well-wisher.'

Tasker punched his desk in frustration. 'What do you make of that?'

'Not good,' Brody said.

'I agree. Who do you think this is?'

'Could be Slaydon.'

Brody nodded. 'It's possible. This letter isn't the work of your common outlaw. Slaydon's a possibility, but this would lose him any standing he has in the community. Would he really be prepared to make himself an outlaw by arranging a kidnapping? Just to get his son freed from jail? Seems unlikely to me.'

Tasker had no answer to that.

'Where is this Falls?' Brody asked.

'It's a waterfall on the Brentwood River, about thirty miles or so south of town. The town's named after it, although I never understood why, since it's so far away.'

'Do you think the outlaws could have got there already?'

'I doubt it, Brody. They took the women in a wagon, couldn't have been pulled by more than two horses. But don't try to think about intercepting them. They would definitely have arrived there by the time you could get

104

there, and if you went barging in, that would most likely get the women killed. And you as well, probably.'

'I wasn't considering it. But I'm trying to think of anything we can do to get more of an advantage.'

'We have to go to the meet. Just me and you and Ricky.'

'But we mustn't get there before three o'clock tomorrow.' Brody paced up and down the office, thinking. Then he stopped abruptly. 'Why don't you ride out to Triple S, see if Slaydon's there? If you can speak to him, you might get a sense of whether he knows anything about it.'

Tasker rubbed his chin. 'Might work at that. And what would you be doing?'

'Obviously, I can't go to Slaydon's ranch with you. Slaydon hates the sight of me. But I thought I might borrow Mikey. He would know the lie of the land around the Falls.'

'You're not thinking of trying some crazy stunt.'

'No. It's a place that I don't know from my afternoon rides. If I can rescue the women without any danger, I will, but I could get an idea of what we're riding into tomorrow.'

Tasker thought about it. 'As long as you're careful. I'll ride out to the Triple S, find out what I can. I can ask Benjy to come and mind the store. Then you can go with Mikey to the Falls.'

CHAPTER ELEVEN

Tasker rode up to the ranch house at the edge of the Triple S spread. An imposing building, standing three stories high, it had a staircase leading to a long veranda in front of its entrance. In front of the staircase, Tasker dismounted and began to climb the stairs, when a man with a rifle came out of the door. Tasker recognized Fred Slaydon, Dan's brother.

'Hold it right there,' Fred said.

'I'm here to see your brother.'

Fred was unimpressed. 'Wait there,' he said, and went back into the house.

Tasker waited. Three windows opened, and rifle barrels protruded from them, pointing directly at him.

Fred returned, and Dan Slaydon followed a couple of paces behind.

'Why are you here, Tasker?' Slaydon called out. He stopped just outside the house's main door and made no further move to come forward.

'I wanted to talk to you.'

'Take off your gun belts, and then we can talk.'

Tasker undid his belts and laid them over his saddle.

'That's fine, Tasker,' Slaydon said. 'You can step away from your horse now and walk . . . slowly. . . up the staircase.'

The sheriff climbed very carefully up the steps. As he reached the top, Slaydon nodded to Fred, who handed his rifle to Slaydon. Fred stepped forward, and without asking, raised Tasker's arms, patted him down, checking for any concealed weapons.

As Fred finished and stepped away, the sheriff said, 'Now is that any way to treat a visitor?'

Slaydon spat, 'You're not welcome here, Tasker. Unless you've brought my boy. Which, since he isn't with you, you haven't done.'

'It's not within my authority to let Rick go. He was caught red-handed at the scene of a murder.'

'He told you he didn't do it.'

The sheriff scoffed. 'If I told you I didn't pick my nose, would you believe me?' The sheriff stuck a finger up his nose.

Slaydon scowled.

Tasker asked, 'Have you done anything about getting a lawyer to help Ricky?'

Slaydon said, 'I sent by telegraph to a firm of lawyers in Tucson. Nobody in Silver Springs will work for me. I advised them to come and force you to let my boy go. They wired back three days ago, and they'll be sending somebody by the noon stage tomorrow.'

'And you'll wait until then before you take any action to get Ricky released?'

107

'Tasker, you know very well that if I decided to take Rick out of your jail, I could come and take him by force.'

Tasker pursed his lips. 'I've heard tell of that sort of thing happening in other towns. Never ends well.'

'I'll speak with the lawyer tomorrow. I'm sure that we'll come up with some solution which will be satisfactory to me and to your over-zealous sense of justice.'

'Which will involve you getting Ricky released, then you'll smuggle him off to Mexico or some such until all the fuss has died down.'

'I had something like that in mind.'

'It might work.' Sheriff Tasker pushed the brim of his Stetson a little lower over his eyes. 'I'd still prefer to see somebody hanged for the murder of Genevieve. And there's also the matter of Stillman.'

'Indeed. Have you made any progress in uncovering the murderer of Mr Stillman?'

'No. Thanks for your concern.'

'I'll be speaking to you tomorrow, after I've discussed matters with the lawyer.'

'Well,' the sheriff said. 'I will bid you good day, Mr Slaydon.'

Tasker strapped his guns back on, then rode off. He never looked back, not even once.

Brody and Mikey rode south, passing the border of the Triple S, then travelling through homesteading country. The late afternoon sun beat down. The trail was good, and Brody remembered the road from driving the stagecoach along it. Then they turned off from the route which led eventually to Silver Springs, and the landscape began to change. Soon they came to a river, and this trail followed its bank, alongside an area of woodland. Another half hour's ride, and Mikey halted, signalling for Brody to do the same.

'We can walk through the woods, and then you'll be able to get a view of the falls.'

'Will it take long to get there?' Brody asked.

Mikey shook his head. 'Should only be about fifteen minutes.'

After tying their horses to a tree, they walked swiftly through the woods, Mikey leading the way with total assurance. He led Brody to a footpath near the bank of the river. Eventually, Brody heard a rushing noise, a loud unending crescendo of water tumbling against rocks. It became deafening, and there was no need for them to be quiet, because little except the rushing water could be heard.

The woodlands thinned as they approached a cliff-edge beside the waterfall. Brody neared the edge, about ten yards from the water, and crouched down to look over the cliff. He saw the water pouring into a wider river, which stretched out into the distance and broadened yet further as it approached the horizon. There was activity on the left bank. There was a wagon, horse still attached to it, and three other horses were hitched to the wagon. Three men stood nearby, casually holding rifles. Brody scanned the area.

'I don't see the women,' Brody shouted. The rushing water meant that there was no chance the outlaws would hear.

Mikey said, 'There's a cave behind the falls, I'm certain they'll be in there.' He was almost screaming, but Brody was only just able to hear him.

'Do you think that we'd be able to rescue them just now?' Brody bellowed.

Mikey shook his head. 'Not a chance. The only way into the cave is a pathway at the bottom of the cliff, near where those men are. We'd have to make our way down there, and they would see us for sure if we got onto that path.'

Brody thought for a moment.

'I'd like to try to get into that cave, make sure that the women are there. Is there an easy way down the cliff?'

'There's a path down to the bottom, about two hundred yards from here.'

'Let's go then.'

They soon reached the narrow pathway, which was just wide enough to walk down with a little care. Brody was glad that he had no fear of heights. The pathway led away from the falls, taking them a good distance from it. There was a jutting rock formation behind and below them which concealed the pathway from the men below. As they descended, the deafening thunder of the falls quietened a little, allowing them to talk at a more normal level.

'Do you think that you could make some kind of distraction, so I can get into the cave without being seen?' Brody asked.

'Reckon so,' Mikey said.

After about fifteen minutes, Brody and Mikey got to the bottom, then turned back towards the falls through another wooded area, which meant that they could walk easily without being spotted. As the woodland thinned, they stopped, and crouched down.

'What do you reckon?' Brody asked.

'Four men, probably. I see three, but there's sure to be a man inside the cave. Maybe another. The wagon could have had two men on it.'

'You got an idea for a distraction?'

'A few gunshots should do it. That'll be loud enough to be heard.'

'Wait until I get into position.'

Mikey drew his gun and thumbed the safety.

'And you'll be able to avoid getting caught?' Brody asked.

'I know this landscape,' Mikey said. 'I grew up on one of the farms not far from here. I used to play hooky from school and spent a lot of time in this area. Nobody knows this ground better than me.'

'Just be careful,' Brody said.

Brody set off towards the pathway, hidden by the trees. He didn't have to worry about stealth because of the noise. After a few yards, he looked back, and was already unable to see Mikey, but he was sure that Mikey could see him. As he reached the path, he paused, taking cover where the beginning of the pathway sloped upwards onto a ledge. Sticking his head above the cover, he saw the three outlaws standing at positions by the bank of the river, looking in the opposite direction.

It was a couple of minutes before anything happened. There were three gunshots. Their piercing cracks

111

were audible even above the rushing noise. Brody saw the outlaws reacting to the sound, looking around and then at each other. He now saw their faces clearly but didn't recognize them. He had thought that they might be some of Slaydon's men, and he had seen several of those in the saloon, but these weren't any of them. Maybe these outlaws had nothing to do with Slaydon. But then why would they want to exchange the women for Rick?

It doesn't make any sense, he thought.

One of the outlaws, a tall burly man, signalled to the others, and they set off in the direction of the shots. Brody waited a moment to make sure that none of them were looking back in the direction of the falls, then set off along the pathway, crouching low, but he needn't have worried. As he got halfway to the falling water, another three shots rang out. He looked over, and the outlaws moved faster towards the source of the shots, not taking the slightest glance backwards. A few more steps, and he was behind the waterfall.

The roar was even more deafening now, almost too loud for Brody to hear himself think. He knew that if he wanted to, he could shout as loudly as he wished, and not be heard by anybody.

There was diffuse sunlight shining through the falling torrent, and a small rainbow which gave additional illumination. A couple of steps further on, Brody came to a cave entrance.

He found a short tunnel, which widened out into a large cavern. It wasn't dark, with illumination being provided by lanterns attached to the walls. There was a protruding rock at one wall, and he stepped up to it, carefully putting his head around to see what was ahead.

It was a cavernous chamber, and the two women were propped up against the wall, tied up. They were dressed as they had been at church, although now dishevelled. They were set about ten feet apart, so that they would be unable to make any physical contact, or talk to each other because of the noise. Incongruously, a man was sitting on a chair, about fifteen feet in front of them, holding a rifle casually. He didn't glance around.

Brody saw no point in attempting a rescue. He had seen the lie of the land, knew that the women were safe for now, and although he was certain that he could best the man guarding them, he doubted he could get them away from their other captors in safety.

He was about to turn back, when Louise looked around and saw him. Her eyes widened but he motioned for her not to react. He knew that she could shout as loudly as she wished and still not be heard over the roaring water, but it was really to indicate that she should make no move which would alert her captor to his presence.

'I'll be back,' he mouthed in an exaggerated fashion. She nodded, almost imperceptibly, to indicate that she understood. Then he waved and headed back to the cave entrance.

Making his way back along the pathway, he looked for any sign of the other outlaws, but they were presumably still searching for the source of the gunshots. He quickly made his way to the woodland and hurried on towards the agreed rendezvous point. When he was nearly there, he saw three men heading in his direction but he ducked into a thicket, and they passed without spotting him.

Arriving at the rendezvous, he looked around for Mikey, but didn't see him. He decided that he could wait a while without too much worry, sure that Mikey's confidence in his ability to conceal himself wasn't misplaced.

As Brody leaned against a tree to make himself more comfortable, a figure dropped in front of him. He was so startled that he drew his gun, then realized that it was Mikey, and holstered it again.

'I take it they couldn't find you.'

'Yep. I climbed up this tree. They walked straight by me and never saw me. Five minutes ago, they walked back again.'

'I saw them a little while ago. Fortunately, they didn't see me.'

'Did you find Miss Adelaide and Miss Louise?'

'I did. There was one guard in the cave, who didn't see me. I decided trying a rescue was too risky. Louise saw me, and I was able to signal to her that I would come back for her. But I couldn't tell her when, because I couldn't get near her. The guard was watching them the whole time.'

'But you'll be able to rescue them tomorrow . . . you and the sheriff?'

'I hope so. We've seen enough here. Let's head back to town.'

*

114

It was mid-evening when Brody and Mikey got back. Tasker was sitting outside his office, keeping an eye on the town.

'Hello, Brody,' Tasker said. 'Did you find where the women are being held?'

'They're in the cave behind the falls. There were three men outside, four horses and a wagon. Thanks to Mikey, I was able to sneak into the cave. Louise and Adelaide were there, guarded by one other man. They seemed to be unharmed.'

'Any idea who these outlaws are?'

'No,' Brody said. 'Never saw any of them before. How did it go with Slaydon?'

'He was his usual charming self.'

'I'll bet.'

'I got the impression that he knows nothing about the women being kidnapped. I asked him what he's going to do about Ricky, and he said that he's sent for a lawyer from Tucson, who'll arrive on the noon stage.'

'Could be a problem for us if Slaydon's not involved in the kidnap. We'll have to take Rick to the rendezvous with the outlaws, otherwise there'll be no chance of res-cuing the women. But if Slaydon isn't involved, he and his lawyer could come here for Rick when we've taken him away.'

'We'll have to come up with some excuse to explain why I'm not here, and Ricky isn't either. We'll need to think about that.'

'I'll meet you here about noon tomorrow. I'll get away from the smithy early, and hopefully by then one of us will have come up with something.'

'You're still going to the smithy? I'd have thought that would be the last thing on your mind.'

'It'll stop me worrying. And physical work helps me think. Want to make a wager on which of us comes up with a plan?'

'No thanks. See you tomorrow, Brody.'

'Good night, boss.'

CHAPTER TWELVE

It was just gone noon when Brody entered the sheriff's office and saw that they had a visitor.

'Hello, Brody,' Tasker said.

Brody nodded, then examined the stranger sitting at the sheriff's desk, dressed in a black frock coat and derby hat. He was aged about forty and had a luxuriant thick black moustache. He also wore a monocle in his right eye and fiddled with it nervously.

'Brody, I'd like you to meet Wilbur Jones,' Tasker said. 'He's a law clerk from Tucson. He's just arrived on the noon stage.'

Brody shook hands with the visitor, who wore a starched, dazzlingly-white shirt with a high collar, and he had a polka-dot necktie, his one apparent concession to frivolity.

'Delighted to meet you,' Brody said. 'I thought that a lawyer was coming and would want to meet with Mr Slaydon first.'

The law clerk shook his head. 'That's my superior, who travelled on the stage with me. Digby Danvers is his name, junior partner in Sutton, Sutton and Danvers of Tucson. Mr Slaydon telegraphed us to request a lawyer to attend due to the fact that his son has been arrested for murder. Mr Fred Slaydon met Mr Danvers when the stage arrived and took him to the Triple S ranch for a conference with the owner.'

Tasker said, 'I'd be obliged, Mr Jones, if you would keep your voice down, because young Ricky Slaydon is in the only operating cell out the back of this office.'

Jones raised his un-monocled eye quizzically.

Tasker chose not to enlighten the law clerk concerning the jailbreak. 'Do go on, Mr Jones,' he said.

'Where was I . . . oh yes. It was the reason for needing a lawyer from Tucson that is the cause of my being here as well as Mr Danvers. The matter needs both of us in attendance, but we're not both needed to discuss the matters concerning the murder charge against the son. So, I've come straight here to you to discuss it.'

Brody saw that the sheriff was getting irritated, his face setting into a frown. Brody too wished that Jones would get on with it. They had to start out soon to the Falls to meet with the outlaws who were holding the women.

Jones stroked his moustache. 'The telegram informed us that Mr Slaydon was in contact with us due to the death of his lawyer in Brentwood Falls, Bradley Stillman.'

'That's correct,' the sheriff said.

'Now a couple of weeks ago, we were visited by Mr Stillman at our offices. He deposited a number of papers with us and stipulated that they were to be opened in the event of his death. We had no expectation that we would be opening the packet so soon.'

Brody said, 'Let me guess. The papers are about Dan Slaydon.'

Jones looked up at Brody. 'Indeed. How did you know?'

'I may not look it, but I'm a qualified lawyer. I'm also a temporary deputy here in town, and Sheriff Tasker asked me to look over Stillman's papers. I was surprised to find that there was nothing relating to Slaydon or the Triple S Ranch, or for the Slaydon Silver Mine. Which I thought very odd.'

Jones nodded and continued. 'When we received Mr Slaydon's communication that Mr Stillman was dead, we immediately opened the papers, and they made for very interesting reading.' Jones paused again and stroked his moustache. 'There were a number of papers pertaining to Mr Slaydon's business dealings, regarding the mine and the ranch. I understand that the mine is long disused. But the papers advised that it had belonged to one Henry Carne . . .'

'That's right,' Brody said.

'. . . and that Carne had left the mine to Stillman in his will. The will further stipulated that if Carne's daughter, Jemima Carne, were to marry Slaydon, she would keep a half-share of the mine, and otherwise she would only get a small bequest of one hundred dollars. There's a document showing her acceptance of the terms. I understand that she took the money, left the town, and went back east.'

'That's right,' Brody said. 'She was my mother.'

Jones' eyes widened, and he gave Brody a hard stare.

'My name is Carne Brody. My mother left Brentwood

119

Falls, and went back to Philadelphia, where she had lived as a child. I take it, Mr Jones, that you have all the documentation here with you.'

'Indeed, I do. And I have to inform you that you were the rightful inheritor of the silver mine.'

'I knew it. My mother told me all about it just before she died, just a few weeks ago.'

'I'm sorry to hear that, Mr Brody. And is your father still with us?'

'Unfortunately, not. He was killed in the war, in a Confederate ambush. But he was a very wealthy man and I got half of his wealth. My mother got the rest, and now that she has died, I've inherited her estate.'

'And yet you look like a working man.'

'I prefer to do manual labour when I can. So, I'm the real heir of the silver mine?'

'Indeed, you are. When Mr Stillman deposited the documents pertaining to Mr Slaydon, he included a notarized affidavit.' Jones paused for effect. 'The affidavit states that Henry Carne's will was a forgery. That Stillman was a party to this fraud. The papers include the real will, in which Henry Carne had left everything to his daughter.'

'That's what my mother told me. I knew that she wasn't lying, but I thought that her memory might be faulty. She was in a lot of pain when she was dying, and her mind might not have been clear.'

'But you didn't really believe that, Mr Brody?'

'No. I came out to Arizona after she died, looking for proof. First, I went to Silver Springs, where she told me that her brother had been living. She said that he would have inherited the mine, but that he died.'

'The affidavit alludes to that. Stillman alleges that Mr Dominic Carne, her brother, was murdered by Dan Slaydon. His affidavit states that Dominic Carne was murdered in the street in Silver Springs, shot in the back. There were no witnesses, and the crime was unsolved. But Stillman stated that he was a witness, that he saw Dan Slaydon do the shooting, and didn't come forward because he feared for his own life.'

Brody knew that this was worse than his mother could have imagined. He knew very little about his uncle. He hadn't known that Uncle Dom had been murdered, until he had made enquiries on his recent visit to Silver Springs.

'Does Slaydon know anything about this affidavit?' Brody asked.

'No,' Jones said. 'Mr Danvers and Messrs Sutton were in two minds about coming to discuss anything at all with Daniel Slaydon. They were certainly going to send me to present this evidence to you. But they decided that they shouldn't turn down business just because the client is an alleged thief and murderer. Indeed, that makes him potentially more profitable.'

Brody turned to Tasker. 'You see why I prefer manual work to practising law.'

Tasker nodded.

'I'm afraid,' Jones said, 'that a lawyer cannot concern himself with justice, not unless he becomes a judge.'

Brody saw that Tasker was getting impatient, pacing up and down, clearly anxious to be done with this. A thought occurred to Brody. 'Mr Jones, I wonder if you would be good enough to assist us in a little subterfuge?'

Jones looked up at Brody.

'It's just that, for reasons I can't go into just now, we have to take Richard Slaydon from his cell this afternoon. I have no doubt that once your Mr Danvers has finished his conference with Mr Slaydon, he will want, at the very least, to interview the prisoner. I ... we ... would be obliged if you could inform Mr Danvers that Rick Slaydon has offered to help us as a material witness in a matter concerning a recent incident at the ruins of the Carne ... Slaydon ... Silver Mine. So, we have had to take him out there this afternoon.'

Jones stroked his moustache. 'Is this matter about the silver mine ... how shall I put it ... is it the truth?'

'Not strictly speaking,' Brody admitted.

'Well in that case, I would be delighted to communicate that to Mr Danvers.' Jones grinned broadly, and Brody thought that he caught a twinkle in the man's eye. 'Sutton, Sutton and Danvers don't pay nearly enough for me to be completely honest with them all the time.'

Tasker spoke up. 'Will you be at the hotel, Mr Jones?'

Jones nodded.

'Benjy!' Tasker called out to the cell corridor.

Benjy popped his head out from behind the curtain hiding the corridor. 'Yes, boss?'

'If Slaydon or a lawyer named Danvers come here this afternoon, you're to refer them to Mr Wilbur Jones at the hotel. That clear, Benjy?'

'Yes, boss.' Benjy disappeared behind the curtain again.

'We'll bid you good day, Mr Jones,' Tasker said.

Jones tipped his hat, adjusted his monocle, and left.

Four horses rode out along the trail towards the falls. There were only three riders, with one of them not really riding, because it was Rick Slaydon, still handcuffed. Rick's horse was tethered to Tasker's, and the spare horse tied to Brody's horse. They rode easily, making good time in the fine afternoon sunshine.

Rick whined the whole time, not understanding where he was being taken, or why. Tasker told him to shut up. Several times.

As they neared the Brentwood River, Brody slipped a look at his pocket watch. He had changed into his 'gentleman' clothing, and so could carry the watch. It was quarter past two.

He hadn't had time to explain his plan to Tasker, but had consulted Mikey last evening, and the deputy had readily agreed. But the sheriff had been within earshot of Rick Slaydon and discussing it in front of the boy would have been a bad idea. The less he knew, the better.

As they neared the woodland a figure was visible, standing waiting, patting his horse. He looked like an eastern gentleman, just like Brody.

'What the hell?' said Tasker, drawing his gun.

'Don't do that, boss,' Brody said. 'It's only Mikey.'

'Mikey? I thought he was sick.'

'No. I came up with a plan. He's dressed like me. In fact, it's one of my suits he's wearing.'

'What are you playing at, Brody?'

'You're going to ride into the outlaws' encampment for the rendezvous. But playing the role of Brody will be

123

our own Mikey.'

'Why didn't you tell me?'

'I thought you might not agree. The plan is that I rescue the women, while you and "Brody" meet with the outlaws.'

'But they'll know it's not you.'

'Will they? The men I saw yesterday were unknown to me. Which means they don't know me.'

'But the note asked for you specifically. They must know who you are.'

'That would have made sense if the kidnapper is Slaydon. But I don't think it is. They'll see Mikey and think that he's me. As long as he doesn't open his mouth.'

'What if they do know you?'

'It's a chance worth taking. We can't trust these outlaws to stick to the deal. My way, at least there's a chance.'

They rode up to Mikey.

'Everything according to plan?' Brody asked.

Mikey nodded.

'I think this might be the most damn fool idea ever,' Tasker said.

'You got a better suggestion?'

Tasker spit, but said, 'It could work at that.'

'Let me get into position, then you can ride in. Allow me five minutes, then approach the outlaws like we're ready to do the trade.'

Tasker nodded assent. Brody turned and set off, sticking to the wooded area until he reached the edge of the pathway to the cave. After a short wait, he saw the riders approach. He ran quickly along the pathway and reached the concealment of the waterfall in moments. He could only hear the rush of falling water and couldn't see what was happening with Tasker and the outlaws. He had to trust that Tasker could keep them occupied.

Entering the cave, he saw that the women were tied up in the same positions as before, but now two outlaws were guarding them. One, the man he had seen the day before, was sitting as then, rifle in hand, resting the barrel over his thighs. The other man had his back to Brody.

Brody pondered the best move.

Tasker stopped as he reached the clearing. He had never seen any of these outlaws before, nor did he recognize any of their faces from wanted posters. He suspected that they weren't planning to exchange the women for Rick Slaydon.

What happened next turned that suspicion into a certainty.

One of the outlaws suddenly raised his rifle and blasted a shot directly at Rick. The lead caught him squarely in the chest, and he fell off his horse.

Tasker's horse reared at the noise, and Rick's riderless horse tethered to it also reared up. Tasker slipped out of the saddle and onto the ground. The rearing horses gave him cover, and he steadied his feet on the ground, drawing both his guns. As the horses rose up again, he was able to fire a shot at the outlaw who had fired at Ricky and hit him in the shoulder.

One of the other outlaws was firing wildly. Tasker

dodged out of the way of the horses and ducked behind a rock. He glanced over at Mikey, who had dismounted and was also running for cover.

Tasker stood up and fired the five remaining shots in the chamber, to give covering fire to allow Mikey to reach safety. Mikey had almost made it, but a slug caught him in the thigh, and he fell sprawling to the ground.

Brody stepped towards the outlaw facing away from him and pushed his gun-barrel hard to the back of the man's neck, thumbing the safety as he did so. With his free hand he also lifted the man's gun from its holster and pressed that one into the man's back.

'Stand very still,' Brody shouted, at the top of his voice. The other outlaw, the man with the rifle, didn't even look around. The roaring of the waterfall prevented the sound of Brody's voice carrying.

'Nod if you can hear me,' Brody shouted.

There was a slight movement of the man's head.

'Start walking . . . slowly.' Brody was screaming at the top of his voice, his lungs almost bursting.

The man started to walk forward. The other outlaw noticed the movement and took his eyes away from the women.

Brody was shielded by the outlaw he had got the drop on. The other outlaw raised his rifle and took aim at his colleague. Then he changed his mind and turned to point the rifle at Adelaide.

Brody knew he had to act quickly. He took the gun in his left hand away from the outlaw's back, aimed at the other man, and fired.

The slug grazed the outlaw's forehead, and blood trickled down his face. Reacting to the pain, he turned the rifle towards Brody. The other outlaw, realizing that his partner in crime would shoot him to get to Brody, made a sudden backwards lunge with his elbow, and caught Brody in the ribs, winding him.

But he had made his move too late. The gunman fired, catching Brody's assailant in the chest, and the man slumped forward to the ground.

Brody doubled up due to the pain in his ribs. The prone outlaw offered next to no cover, but Brody ducked down behind him anyway. Despite the pain, Brody had only moments in which to act. He fired both guns.

He barely heard the noise of the shots above the sound of rushing water.

The bullet caught the outlaw's arm, and he dropped the rifle. He fell backwards, but landed against the cavern wall, which kept him upright. He tried to grab for the rifle, but it had fallen just beyond his reach, then realized that he still had a gun in his holster, so drew it, and aimed at Louise.

He got off a shot. Brody shouted – 'No!' – and took aim again, not even looking to see if Louise had been hit and fired three shots in quick succession.

One of the shots caught the outlaw in the forehead, and he fell with the impact. Brody scrambled over to him, and kicked him in the chest several times, enraged, but stopped when he realized that the man was dead.

Then he rushed to the women and was relieved to see that neither had been hit.

*

Tasker returned fire at the outlaw who had shot Mikey, but the man ducked for cover behind the wagon.

Tasker ran towards his deputy, grabbed him by the arms, and pulled him roughly to safety behind the rocks, unable to worry about his condition because the outlaws recommenced shooting at them.

The four horses that Tasker and Mikey had brought to the rendezvous were still rearing up wildly, tied together in twos, kicking up dust, making it difficult for Tasker to see anything. He put his head above the rock and fired rapidly towards the wagon. Return fire whizzed above his head. One shot caught his hat and blew it off his head.

He ducked down again and brought his attention to Mikey.

'Are you hit bad?' he asked.

'Guess not,' Mikey said. 'Just a graze. But there's a hole in Brody's second-best coat now, and it's covered in blood. I reckon he's going to be mighty mad at me.'

Tasker laughed. 'That's the least of our worries right now.'

Tasker reloaded, stood up, and fired once more towards the wagon. He couldn't tell if his shots were having any effect. The dust stirred up by the horses was preventing him from seeing anything.

Tasker ducked down again. 'Mikey, can you shoot?' Tasker asked.

'I don't think so,' Mikey said. 'It's my shooting arm that got hit.'

Tasker said, 'There are still two outlaws out there, and they might have reinforcements nearby.'

'Well, it's been nice knowing you, boss.'

'Mikey! Don't give up on me. We've got out of worse scrapes than this one.'

Mikey scratched his head. 'When?'

'Come to think of it, none of them has been worse than this.'

Tasker turned and put his head above cover again. He fired four shots, then ducked down again. 'Visibility's improving.'

'Then we're done for.'

'Come on, Mikey. Never say die. I think you can shoot with your left hand.'

'Just because you can, boss, doesn't mean that I can.'

'Then why do you wear two guns?'

'I was just copying you. When I need to use my left-handed gun, I holster my other one, and switch hands.'

'Time to try a different way, then. What have you got to lose?'

'My life.'

'Hell, you're probably going to lose that anyway.' Tasker chuckled. 'I'm going to make a run for those trees over there. When I start going, I want you to fire as many shots as you can, to cover me. I'll leave you a gun, so that'll give you eighteen shots before you have to reload.'

Tasker started to run, crouching low. He heard shots behind him but didn't look back. He lost count after seven. There was no way to tell how many of those shots were Mikey's. He kept running and found some trees that gave him cover. He headed behind a large tree-trunk and turned. There were two outlaws hidden behind the wagon, but one wasn't covered from this new angle.

Tasker took aim and fired.

The outlaw fell.

Tasker fired again, hoping for a lucky shot that would get the other outlaw, but it missed.

Then he squeezed the trigger yet again, but the gun jammed.

He squeezed the trigger twice more. Nothing. The mechanism had failed.

The outlaw was staring straight at him. The man realized that Tasker could no longer shoot at him. He cursed his decision to leave his other gun for Mikey to use.

Mikey was no longer shooting. Tasker glanced over to where Mikey was hiding against the rock, and saw that he was trying to load one of the guns but was struggling to do it because of his injured arm. The outlaw realized that nobody was shooting at him now and started to come closer to get a better shot.

Brody untied Louise. The knot was tight, but he took the knife he carried in his boot and frayed the rope enough to loosen it. Louise then put her arms around Brody, pulled him towards her, and gave him a sensuous kiss. Brody returned it fiercely, but briefly, then turned to Adelaide. The knot was a bit looser around the schoolteacher's hands, and she was quickly freed.

Brody motioned for them to move towards the cave entrance. They got to their feet, dusted themselves down as best they could, and the three of them exited the cave into the daylight.

Brody surveyed the scene and saw two outlaws injured or dead. Another was walking towards Tasker, gun in hand. He saw no sign of Mikey.

Tasker turned to run.

The outlaw raised his gun.

Brody fired off three rounds, knowing otherwise that Tasker was done for. The third shot hit the outlaw in the back. He spasmed and hit the dust.

Brody saw Tasker turn to look, then start running towards them. As he neared the downed outlaw, the man's hand reached out and caught him by the ankle, tripping him up. Adelaide was past Brody in an instant, raising her skirts to allow her to run faster. Brody looked around at Louise, who motioned for him to follow Adelaide.

Brody ran, and managed to overtake the school teacher. Brody could see that Tasker wasn't injured, just winded where the outlaw had pulled him down. Brody helped Tasker to his feet, then Adelaide was upon the sheriff, grabbing hold of him.

Brody turned to the outlaw, who was staring up at the sky. His mouth was moving, as if he wanted to say something. Brody leaned over the man, trying to catch what he was saying.

'Ishmael!' the outlaw whispered. Then he chuckled, as if he hadn't a care in the world. The laugh turned into a sputtering cough, which forced blood into his mouth. Then he died.

'What the hell happened here?' Brody asked.

'Beats me if I know,' Tasker said.

Brody looked around. 'Where's Rick Slaydon?'

'The outlaws killed him.'

'Why would they do that?'

'Don't know,' Tasker said.

'That outlaw said something before he died. Ishmael.'

'Looks like we've been suckered. Your friend Ishmael wanted us out of town.'

'What for?' asked Brody.

'We'll find out when we get there.'

'Just one thing that worries me,' Brody said.

'What's that?' Tasker asked.

'What is old man Slaydon going to do when he finds out we've let his son get killed?'

CHAPTER THIRTEEN

They arrived back in town in the early evening. Brody and Tasker had rounded up the horses, their own and those of the outlaws, and had taken the outlaws' wagon, using it to transport the corpses. Tasker and Brody had even taken the time to collect the bodies from the cave. Mikey and Adelaide sat on the wagon's driving bench, with Adelaide driving because of Mikey's injury.

Louise insisted that she ride a horse, even though she wasn't suitably dressed. She ripped her dress to be able to ride astride, even though it had cost a hundred dollars.

Adelaide pulled the wagon to a halt outside the undertaker's shop. Old man Raleigh was just locking up for the night, but he rubbed his hands with glee when he saw that providence had brought him more business, making it worth his while to stay open a bit longer.

Tasker suggested that the women should stay at the hotel for the time being. But Brody had an alternative idea.

'Will, I think that would be asking for trouble. We should put it about that they are staying in the hotel, but

133

they should go somewhere else, where nobody would think of looking for them.'

'Why should we do that?' Louise asked.

'When Slaydon finds out what happened to his son, things could get very ugly. He'll blame us, and he'll think that you two are involved.'

Tasker said, 'He's capable of anything. All four of us are in danger.'

Adelaide reached out and took Tasker's hand, squeezed it. 'Where should we go?' she asked.

Brody pondered, then had a realization. 'Stillman's house.'

'That's an idea, Brody,' Tasker said. 'It's way on the other side of town. None of the Slaydon gang would think of it. And it's set out a ways from anybody else, so nobody would know you were there, Addie.'

The women readily agreed. Louise suggested that they would take Mikey to the hotel, send for the doctor for him, and arrange for the hotel staff to check them in. They would wait until dark, and then sneak out to Stillman's house.

Having settled this, the women and Mikey went to the hotel, and Tasker and Brody rode on. As they got further up the street, it became obvious why Ishmael had tricked them into leaving town. There was a cloud of dust hanging over the bank. They approached, and found Benjy sitting outside the premises, wielding a rifle.

Tasker jumped off his horse and went to Benjy. 'I see we've had some trouble.'

'Sure have,' Benjy said. 'Bank robbers. But they didn't come in the bank and threaten anybody. They dynamited the back wall and stole the safe. Got clean away.'

'Any witnesses?'

Benjy shook his head. 'Nobody saw the robbers. I had a look around after the bank manager reported the robbery, and I found this.'

Benjy fished a crumpled note out of his pocket and handed it to Tasker. Tasker opened it up and read it. 'Call me Ishmael,' he read aloud.

'So that's what this was about,' Brody said.

Tasker spat, 'A trick by Ishmael to get us out of town.'

Brody nodded. 'This wasn't about freeing Rick Slaydon at all.'

'And the first thing that the outlaws at the falls did was kill Ricky,' Tasker said.

'Ishmael ordered them to do that. Then to kill us.'

'Ishmael must have some connection to the Slaydons. A grudge against them, maybe?'

Brody said nothing.

Benjy had a puzzled look on his face. 'Sheriff, did you say that Rick Slaydon is dead?'

'Yes. The outlaws killed him as soon as we approached them.'

'Dan Slaydon came looking for you this afternoon, like you said he would, with a lawyer named Danvers. I told him what you said, to speak to that law clerk.'

Tasker said, 'He'll blame me for the death of his son.'

Benjy chuckled. 'If I was you, boss, I'd leave town right away. And never come back.'

'I was thinking of retiring anyway. But I did have a mind to settle down nearby. Addie wants to make an honest man of me.'

'As if you weren't an honest enough man already . . .'
Benjy rubbed his belly, still sore from his injuries. Then
he looked around. 'What's happened to Mikey?'

'He got injured in the shootout at the falls. Addie and
Lou took him to the hotel. He needs some doctoring, but
he should be all right. Won't be much use to us for a
while, though.'

'Tarnation,' Benjy said. 'Just when we need to be at full
strength. I'm not going to be much use to you either.'

Tasker turned to Brody. 'I guess it's just you and me,
then. I hope you're not one who runs away from a fight.'

'Not me,' Brody said. 'I'm sorry that Rick is dead, even
though he was no good, and he killed one of the. . . .'
Brody paused. 'Wait a minute. This whole thing has been
a set-up. Rick didn't kill Genevieve.'

Tasker gave Brody a hard stare. 'He didn't?'

'No. The story he told us was true. About the man
coming out of the closet and slitting her throat.'

'But it was preposterous.'

'That's why you didn't believe it. Think abut it. Rick
was too dumb to make up a story like that. If he'd done
the killing, he'd have confessed to it.'

'Then who did it?' Tasker asked.

'Ishmael.'

'I don't believe it.' The sheriff shook his head.

'It makes sense,' Brody said. 'He wanted Rick to be
arrested for the killing, then he kidnapped Louise and
Adelaide, so he could stage that phony hostage
exchange. And he must have killed Stillman too, because
he knew what would happen.'

'What?'

'That the lawyers in Tucson would give the game away about Slaydon's past. To make us think that Slaydon would be desperate enough to kidnap the women in order to free his son. He must have had some grudge against the Slaydons, and Stillman.'

'But how would Ishmael have known about Stillman's dealings with the Tucson lawyers?' Tasker asked.

Brody shrugged. 'We don't know anything about him, except that he's unusually intelligent for an outlaw. He could be connected to Slaydon, to Stillman, maybe even the lawyers in Tucson. He could be blackmailing them.'

Tasker said, 'That's all supposition. Could be true, but you would have a hard time proving it.'

'Probably,' Brody said, 'but I feel it in my gut that Ishmael is behind it. What are you going to tell Slaydon about Rick?'

'The truth.'

'He'll want revenge. And against us, rather than the people who did it.'

'I shot the man who did it. His corpse is with the undertaker now.'

'But you didn't get the man who told him to do it. Ishmael.'

'We might never get him,' Tasker said. 'If you're right, he's been one step ahead of us all the way.'

'What do you think our chances are against Slaydon?'

'Pretty slim. He's got a lot of men on his ranch. I wouldn't say that they're loyal to him, but they'll do as he says. He rules by fear.'

'Any chance of help from the townspeople?' Brody asked.

Tasker shook his head. 'None at all.'

'Can't ask Benjy to fight, and Mikey won't be able to.'

'Just the two of us, then. I'm sick of being a lawman.'

'I didn't much like it either,' Brody said. 'It's great when everybody's law-abiding, but human nature being what it is, a lot of people aren't.'

'We're safe for now,' Tasker said. 'Slaydon still thinks his son is alive. But you know how he's going to react when he finds out that we took his son to his death.'

Brody rubbed his chin. 'I think I may have an idea. It might give us a chance.'

'Slaydon will bring at least twenty men with him to get his revenge, maybe more. What chance do the two of us have against two dozen men?'

'I'll tell you on the way to your office. We need to get ready.'

Tasker and Brody waited. Brody had explained to Tasker what he had in mind, and Tasker thought it was crazy, but was unable to think of any better option.

They didn't have to wait for long.

After a few minutes, Slaydon flung the door open, and barged into the office. A stout, bespectacled man followed close by, and entering shortly after him was Wilbur Jones, the law clerk. It was obvious to Tasker and Brody that the stranger was the lawyer Digby Danvers, but Slaydon wasn't interested in the niceties of bothering to introduce him.

'Where the hell is my boy?' Slaydon demanded.

'Well now . . .' Tasker hesitated.

'He's dead,' Brody said.

Slaydon was about to speak further, when he suddenly turned and looked at Brody. The colour drained from his face. Then he flew into a rage.

'Who the blazes are you?' he raged at Brody. 'You're just the town blacksmith.'

'I'm also a sworn-in deputy. And a qualified lawyer. And your son is still dead.'

'How did this happen?'

Tasker spoke up. 'Some outlaws kidnapped Miss Summers and Miss Delaware. They said that they wanted to exchange them for Ricky. At first we thought it was you . . .'

'An outrageous slur. How dare you!'

'Well, who else would have wanted Ricky in exchange for the women?' Tasker asked.

Slaydon's face convulsed. 'What happened?' he asked, his voice beginning to break with grief.

'We took Ricky to the meet, which was out by the falls. As soon as we approached the outlaws, they shot him. He didn't stand a chance.'

Slaydon stared hard at Tasker, and then at Brody. 'Yet you escaped unharmed. I don't believe it.'

'We were lucky,' Tasker said. 'And Mikey did get injured.'

'That's none of my concern,' Slaydon said. 'You're both liars, and you murdered my boy. You deserve to die for this.'

Danvers, the lawyer, began to show agitation when he heard his client talking in this manner. 'Mr Slaydon,' he said, 'I would strongly advise you . . .'

Slaydon shouted at him. 'You shut up. If you're not

going to help me prosecute these . . . these . . . criminals, then you're fired.'

Tasker drew his gun and pointed it at Slaydon, just as Brody had suggested.

Brody also drew his gun, stepped swiftly towards Slaydon, and relieved him of his revolver, slipping it easily out of its holster.

Slaydon was enraged. 'What is this? What are you doing?'

'Brody, it was your idea,' Tasker said. 'Would you like to do the honours?'

'Certainly.' Brody nodded. 'Mr Slaydon. We're going to have to lock you up in this jail. For your own good. Until you calm down and see reason.'

'I'll rip you apart, you pipsqueak,' Slaydon thundered.

Brody gave a low laugh, seemingly unimpressed by the threat.

Tasker said, 'Come along now, Slaydon. If you don't move into the cell right now, of your own accord, we're going to carry you and throw you in.'

Slaydon turned to the lawyer. 'Danvers, you can't allow them to do this. I'm ordering you . . .'

Danvers shrugged, and said, 'But you've fired me.'

'I'll get even with you, every one of you.' Slaydon scowled. But he walked into the cell by himself, haughty and proud, not wishing to be manhandled by Tasker and Brody. Once Slaydon was in the cell, Tasker locked it.

'I'll be wanting to speak to a lawyer.'

'That's going to take some time,' Tasker said. 'You've fired Mr Danvers. The only lawyer in town is dead, remember?'

140

'Not counting me, of course,' Brody said. 'And I'm not going to prosecute myself.'

Slaydon blustered and raged, but there was nothing he could do.

Tasker sighed and walked away from the cell. Brody followed.

The law gentlemen from Tucson bid them good night.

Brody and Tasker sat outside the office the next afternoon, watching out for visitors from the Triple S.

There had been little sleep for Brody last night because he had gone to the hotel to help Louise and Adelaide sneak away to Stillman's house, and he had stayed with them until they had settled for the night. He was sure that no-one had seen them as they made their way there, and he knew he hadn't been followed on his return to the hotel.

Benjy was inside the jail, having the task of keeping an eye on Slaydon, and refusing all his demands. This delighted him, since he had once worked as a ranch hand for Slaydon and detested him. The feeling would have been mutual if Slaydon had ever given Benjy any thought at all.

'I have to admit that you were right about locking Slaydon up, Brody. I'd never have dared.'

'That's because you're impressed by wealth, Will. You let it affect your judgement. I'm never impressed by money, not even my own. I judge everybody by the temper of their character, not by how much money they have.'

'Easy for you to say,' the sheriff said. 'I've never had very much.'

'I've got a lot, but I seldom use any of it. It's there for me if I need it, which isn't very often.'

Two men rode in along the street, slowing as they approached the sheriff.

'Here comes trouble,' Tasker said. 'Fred and Dave. Slaydon's brothers.'

The men dismounted. Fred approached the sheriff, while Dave hitched the horses.

'Sheriff, my brother didn't come home last night.'

'Is that right, Fred?' the sheriff said.

'There's some crazy rumour that my nephew is dead, and that you've arrested my brother.'

'It's true that Ricky is dead. I haven't exactly arrested your brother, but I did lock him up.'

'Will you let him go?'

'Nope. Wouldn't be a good idea.'

'Why's that?'

Brody spoke up. 'Because he'd get a gang of you together to come into town and kill us. Don't know about the sheriff, but I don't plan to die any time soon.'

Fred stared at Brody. 'And who might you be, stranger?'

'The name's Carne Brody.'

'Carne?'

'You may have heard of my grandfather, Henry Carne. And my mother.'

Fred Slaydon spit on the ground, then swore. 'Never knew Jemima Carne had a son.'

'She didn't when you knew her. And I never knew until recently that she had a silver mine that your brother stole from her.'

'Can't prove nothing.'

'That's what you think.'

Fred Slaydon turned to the sheriff. 'Can we see our brother?'

'Certainly,' the sheriff said. 'Provided you check your weapons with my deputy here.' Tasker nodded in the direction of Brody.

'I'd be obliged if you would hand me your weapons.' Brody drew his gun to indicate that this wasn't a request.

They reluctantly took off their gun belts and handed them to Brody. The sheriff checked them for concealed weapons, then let them enter the office.

Tasker and Brody followed.

The brothers began a whispered conversation, and the lawmen couldn't hear what was being discussed. Brody knew that if they tried to get into a position where they could hear the discussion, the talking would stop.

After about fifteen minutes or so, Fred approached Tasker.

'My brother has said that he'll make no trouble if you let him go.'

'I don't think I can do that.'

'You're making a big mistake.'

'It's my mistake to make.'

'Then we won't be able to answer for the consequences,' Fred said.

Tasker said, 'I could lock you two in with your brother.'

'You won't though. Some of our employees at Triple S are mighty useful with guns. They have orders about what to do if we don't return.'

Brody was about to say something, but a look from

143

Tasker silenced him.

'We'd be obliged if you would return our guns,' Fred continued.

'Certainly,' the sheriff said, and nodded to Brody.

Brody handed them their gun belts, they strapped them on, and left.

Benjy stood in the doorway and trained a rifle on them as they rode away, just in case.

CHAPTER FOURTEEN

Evening, and Tasker and Brody sat outside the office, watching the street.

'What do you think Dan told his brothers?' Brody asked.

Tasker said, 'To bust him from jail.'

'And to use the persuasive power of lead to do it. Why didn't you lock up Fred and Dave while they were here, and unarmed?'

'I thought about it. But while you were watching the brothers talking, I was looking across the street. There were four more of Slaydon's men outside the hotel. I figured they would attack if none of the Slaydons came back out. Letting Fred and Dave go allows us time to prepare for a siege.'

'How do you think they'll work it?' Brody asked.

'They'll ride into town early in the morning with as many guns as they can muster. What I'm going to do is barricade this office best I can, make it as hard for them as possible. Fortunately, Anders has finished the repairs on the jail wall, so attack from behind isn't likely.'

'I'll ride out to Stillman's house, check on Louise and Adelaide. Then I'll go back to the hotel, try to get some sleep.'

Brody returned to the sheriff's office early, before sun-up. The door was locked, and the windows were all covered with wood, apart from a couple of spaces though which a gun barrel could be inserted.

Brody knocked on the door. 'Will, it's Brody.'

Tasker let him in. 'Were the women all right?'

'They were having some supper when I got there. Louise is getting antsy, though. She doesn't like being in town and letting her understudy perform at the theatre instead of her.'

Tasker shook his head. 'We don't have time to worry about that now. It won't be long before Slaydon's men get here.'

'What do we do then?'

'Kill them. Or die.'

'I vote for kill them,' Brody said.

About an hour later, Slaydon's men rode into town, led by Fred and Dave.

As his brother had advised him, Fred was to attempt to find Louise Delaware and Adelaide Summers. An easily-bribed bellboy in the hotel had informed their men the previous night that the women were staying there. Fred had no way of knowing that the bellboy had been ordered to lie to them. He sent Tom Durden to find them.

Durden returned a few minutes later. 'They checked out, Mr Slaydon, sir.'

Fred spat, 'Did you look for them?'

'Yes. They're gone.'

'Then we're going to have to do it without them.'

Fred left his horse with one of the men, and approached the sheriff's office, rifle in hand.

'Tasker,' he shouted. 'I know you're in there. Let my brother go and there'll be no more trouble.'

'Not a chance!' Tasker shouted from inside.

'Then we'll take him by force,' Fred shouted.

'You can try,' Tasker shouted back.

'Come on, Tasker. You don't stand a chance. It's just you and that blacksmith.'

Fred waited. There was no reply.

'Last warning, Tasker,' Fred shouted.

Still no reply.

Fred turned and walked back to his men. When he reached them, he gave a signal, and the men fired several rounds at the sheriff's office. The sound of gunfire filled the street. Slug after slug impacted the wooden door and the covered-up windows.

It wasn't long before all the guns were emptied.

While the men were reloading, Fred Slaydon shouted, 'You ready to surrender yet, Tasker?'

The reply was a brief volley of shots, Tasker and Brody firing through the gaps in the barricade. One of Slaydon's men was hit in the chest and fell to the ground with a scream.

Fred was about to signal a second attack on the sheriff's office, when there was a single shot which downed another of his men. But this man fell forward, hit in the back. This attack was from the other side of the street. Most of the men turned and ran towards the boardwalk which lined the entrance to the saloon, so that they couldn't be attacked from behind.

Fred turned, and looked up at the roof of the theatre, and spotted somebody carrying a rifle. He was certain from the glimpse of long hair that it was a woman. A shot came, sending up dust just inches in front of him, and he ducked for cover behind a wagon. He motioned to his brother, who was at his side in moments.

He said, 'I'm sure that's one of the women. Go get her. Alive.'

Dave ran to the side of the theatre, to the outside stairway which led up to the roof, and ascended.

Fred decided to wait to see what Dave found. They could waste a lot more ammunition firing at the sheriff's office, and still fail to free his brother.

He risked leaving the spot where he had cover, found a position on the boardwalk about twenty yards south of the entrance to the sheriff's office, and looked up again at the rooftop. At first there was nothing moving, but soon Dave was silhouetted in the morning sun. The crack of a rifle-shot gave him an anxious moment, but he was relieved to see that Dave didn't flinch. Then Dave had the woman's hands in his fist, and the rifle dropped from her grasp. Dave punched her on the jaw, and then dragged her away from the roof edge.

A couple of minutes later, Dave brought Louise Delaware across the street to Fred. She had a bruise on her cheek, and her left eye was beginning to puff up. She spit on Fred and used unladylike language.

Ignoring her, Fred asked, 'Where's the other bitch?'

'Didn't see her,' Dave said.

Fred grabbed Louise by the arm, pulling her out into the street. He put his gun to her head, pressing it hard into her temple. Her eyes flashed with defiance.

'Hey, Sheriff!' shouted Fred. 'We've got your blacksmith's fine little whore here. Sorry we couldn't find your stuck-up schoolmarm, but this'll have to do.'

He waited for a response.

When none came, he continued. 'You have two minutes to bring my brother out here, or else Brody's little tart will get a piece of lead in her brain.' He paused. 'Do you hear me, Tasker?'

No response.

'Do you hear me, Tasker?' he repeated.

'I hear you,' Tasker shouted. 'We're coming out.'

There was a slight delay, then the door was unbolted. It swung open, but there was nobody in the doorway. Fred signalled to his men, who raised their guns.

Slaydon was in the doorway, wrists handcuffed behind his back, Tasker holding a gun to his head. Tasker shoved the rancher forward roughly, pushing him down the two steps into the street. Brody followed them, with guns in both hands.

Tasker stopped, yanking roughly at Slaydon's arms. Brody stepped forward and stood beside them.

Two more gunshots pierced the morning air.

Two of Slaydon's men fell.

Fred looked around but couldn't see where the shots had come from. Had the schoolteacher found a different vantage point? His men also looked around nervously. Fred worried that this could end badly after all. And Dan had said it would be easy. . . .

Dan Slaydon spoke up. 'Let's get this over with, Tasker.'

Tasker said, 'Fred, let Miss Delaware go, and then we'll let your brother free.'

'Call off your other shooters first,' Fred shouted.

'We don't have any other shooters.'

'Then who shot our men?'

'Don't know. Maybe you have other enemies.'

Fred scoffed. 'And they just happen to be here at this moment . . .'

Another shot rang out from across the street. Dan Slaydon caught the slug in his forehead and fell backwards.

'NO!' shouted Fred. 'No!'

Worried for Louise, Brody fired instinctively. His bullet hit Fred in the shoulder, sent him lurching backwards. Louise got free of him and ran towards Brody.

She embraced Brody tightly, but he made sure he had one hand free, because it was still uncertain how this was going to end.

Tasker saw that Dan Slaydon had the glassy stare of a dead man. He stepped forward to look at Fred, who was writhing in agony, and could no longer lead the men.

Tasker shouted so that all the Slaydon men could hear. 'OK, you men. This is over. If you drop your guns now, and leave town, we'll say no more about your involvement in this. I know that you're basically decent men.'

For a moment, nothing happened.

Then Dave Slaydon removed his gun belt and dropped it to the ground. He signalled to the other men, and they followed suit.

Adelaide came running down the street, carrying a rifle, raced to Tasker, and clutched at him fiercely. She kissed him on the cheeks, then firmly on the mouth.

Tasker flushed and turned again to Slaydon's men. 'We'll have to arrest Fred and Dave, but the rest of you are free to go. We'll return your weapons to the ranch in a few days. You can take your injured and dead with you.'

Tasker watched as the men started to leave, as relieved as they were that there was to be no further trouble today.

Tasker said, 'That was a damn fool thing to do, Addie. You could have been killed.'

'So could you, Will,' she replied.

'And what were you thinking when you shot Dan Slaydon?'

'But I didn't. My position was on the roof of the jail. I could have shot him, but it would have got him in the back of the head. And you were so close to him that I didn't dare risk it. Whoever shot him was on the other side of the street.'

Tasker frowned. 'If you didn't shoot him, who did?'

CHAPTER FIFTEEN

Brody lay in bed at the hotel, bone-tired, relieved that it was finally over. But he struggled to sleep. It didn't help that Louise lay beside him.

He tossed and turned through the hours of darkness. As dawn began to lighten the sky, he finally dozed off.

'Brody,' a man's voice said.

He woke with a start, reached for his gun hooked over the bedpost, but it was no longer there. He saw that Louise was gone too.

He sat up in bed, looked at the intruder.

Ishmael.

'What have you done with Miss Delaware?' Brody demanded.

'Nothing,' Ishmael said. 'I waited until she had gone before I came in here.'

'She wouldn't have gone without waking me,' Brody said.

'Apparently she did. I waited until I saw her going into the theatre before I decided to pay you a visit.'

'What time is it?'

'About noon.'

'What do you want?'

'Just to be neighbourly. I thought you might want to thank me.'

Brody frowned. 'What for?'

'Killing Dan Slaydon.'

'So, it was you . . .'

'Yep. If ever a man needed killing, it was him. I wasn't too impressed with your plan for stopping him getting his revenge on you for letting Ricky die . . .'

'You were the one who killed Rick Slaydon.'

'Not me personally. It was my men. I should really hold a grudge against you for killing so many of them, but I can't. I like you, Brody.'

'Much obliged,' Brody said sarcastically. 'I understand about you wanting to rob the bank. You're a criminal, that's what you do. But was all the killing really necessary?'

'Not all of it. Sometimes I kill people because I'm paid to do it. Sometimes because they need killing. And sometimes . . .'

Brody sensed that Ishmael was taunting him, mocking him.

'And sometimes?' Brody asked, because Ishmael was holding the pause too long.

'Sometimes I just like it.'

'It was you who killed Genevieve, wasn't it?'

'Sure. I wanted Rick to be arrested for the killing. So that when I kidnapped the women you would agree to come and trade Rick for them.'

'An innocent woman had to die just so you could rob a bank.'

'She was no innocent. I knew her from before . . .'

'Before what?'

Before I took the name Ishmael. She did some very bad harm to somebody I was fond of, back in Texas.'

'So, you're from Texas?'

'I didn't say that.'

'Why did your men have to kill Rick?'

'Because I didn't like him.'

'Why didn't you like him?'

'Same reason I don't like any of his family.'

'And why's that?'

'I'll tell you sometime, when I get to know you better.'

'And you killed Stillman?'

'Yep. Didn't like him either.'

'But you like me.'

'I do. And that's why I'm going to let you live. And Tasker too,' Ishmael said. 'I shouldn't like him. Never had much truck with lawmen, but he's all right.'

'What are you going to do now?' Brody asked.

'Ride off into the sunset.'

'Just like that?'

'Yep. I'll spend my ill-gotten gains while they last, and when they've gone I'll try to get some more.'

'Your luck will run out some time.'

'Hasn't yet.'

'Where did you put my gun?' Brody asked.

Ishmael laughed. 'I put it in your closet. You can get it when I leave.'

'Very kind, I'm sure.'

'Oh, there's just one thing. I can't trust you not to raise the alarm. So, I'm going to have to tie you to the bed before I go.'

'What? I thought you liked me.'

'I don't like you that much, Mr Carne Brody.'

As Ishmael tied him up, Brody wondered how it was that Ishmael knew his name.

Louise came back an hour later, to find Brody tied and gagged. She released him quickly.

'What happened, Brody?' she asked.

'It was Ishmael. He was very neighbourly, except for the tying-up part. He confessed to killing the prostitute and Stillman, and that his men had killed Rick Slaydon. He also told me that he was the man who shot Dan Slaydon.'

'I suppose I should be grateful to him.'

'It still could have ended badly if I hadn't acted quickly to shoot Fred.'

'I'm even more grateful to you, then,' she said, and kissed him firmly.

'So, what now?' she asked.

'I don't know. I'd love to stay with you, but I don't think you're ready to settle down to be a home-maker.'

'I don't think you're the settling-down kind either, Carne Brody.'

'My name isn't a secret any more.'

'I thought you might be exaggerating when you said you were a rich man.'

'Understating it, perhaps. And I'm going to be even richer now.'

'Why's that?'

'We have evidence that Dan Slaydon forged my grand-father's will. There's no doubt that Henry Carne had left his silver mine to his only living relative, his daughter, and I'm her heir. Because the mine is played out now, the only way that Slaydon's heirs can compensate me for the false disinheritance is to forfeit his ranch to me. I discussed this with the lawyer from Tucson over dinner here at the hotel last night.'

'Would you settle down to ranching? I could see myself as a rancher's wife. I wouldn't give up show business, though.'

'Mighty tempting, Louise, when you put it like that. But I'm not ready to put down roots yet, certainly not as a rancher. I've worked on ranches. As a cow hand in Montana, and as a ranch foreman in Wyoming. I get bored if I work at one thing too long.'

'So, you're going to be moving on?'

'Afraid so. If you gave up performing in the theatre, I would be very tempted . . .'

'I'll not be performing forever. I'm planning to retire in a few years.'

'Then maybe I'll come back someday.'

'What will you do with the ranch meantime?'

'I've got an idea.'

A couple of days later, Brody stepped into the sheriff's office. Tasker was at his desk, and Benjy was at the armoury cupboard, cleaning the rifles.

'Hello, Will,' Brody said.

'Hi, Brody. Come to do a little stint as deputy?' Tasker asked.

'Nope. Come to hand in my badge.'

'I never gave you a badge.'

'Metaphorical badge, then. I've decided to be moving on.'

'Sorry to hear that, Brody. When will you go?'

'Just as soon as I've made the arrangements with Danvers. In effect, I'm Slaydon's heir. Slaydon defrauded my mother's inheritance. He left everything to Ricky, but in the event of Ricky's . . . demise, it reverts to Fred. So Fred has to compensate me. How is Fred, by the way?'

'Doc Stephens patched him up. Then I let him go home. He's basically a decent man, led astray by his brother.'

Brody smiled. 'How would you like to have a school-teacher for a wife?'

'I'd like it fine. But I haven't got enough money to retire from the law.'

'How would you like to run a ranch?'

'I can't afford it.'

'I own a ranch now, or at least I will when Danvers completes the paperwork. Don't like the name Triple S. Maybe change it to Carne Plains Ranch. I'd like you to manage it for me.'

Tasker whistled.

Brody said, 'Of course, if you'd rather not, I could always offer it to Benjy.'

Benjy looked up from the rifle barrel he was cleaning. 'I'll do it, Brody,' he said.

Tasker said, 'Shut up, Benjy.' Then he turned to Brody. 'You're serious?'

'Absolutely.'

'Would you pay me?'

'You can have seventy per cent of the profits. Minus a peppercorn rent . . .'

'A pepper what?'

'It's a legal term for a very low rent. Should be one peppercorn a year, but I don't think anybody grows black pepper in Arizona. So instead of that, I thought you could pay me five cents a year.'

'Always knew you were crazy, Brody.'

'Bank it for me, and my cut of the profits. I'll be back in a couple of years or so, find out how it's going.'

'Then I accept,' Tasker said.

'I'll have Danvers and Jones draw up the contract before they head back to Tucson. On one condition . . .'

Tasker looked puzzled. Brody said, 'Get yourself down to the schoolhouse immediately, and get Adelaide Summers to agree to a date for your wedding and get her to make it soon. I can't leave before the ceremony, because you'll be needing a best man.'

Tasker's jaw dropped open, then it closed again, and he stood up with a firmness of purpose. 'Benjy, hold the fort. I'm going out for a while.'

'Yes, boss.'

Tasker got up from his desk, shook Brody by the hand, and hurried off to the schoolhouse.

Two days after the wedding, Brody left the hotel early in the morning. He walked down the street to the livery stable to collect the palomino and the pack mule that he had bought from Tex Sumpter.

Tex had the horses out waiting for him.

'Brody, I'm sorry to lose you. I don't know where I'm going to find somebody as good as you for the smithy.'

Brody said, 'Sorry, Tex. You knew this was only going to be temporary.'

'I wish you'd stay, though.'

'Got to move on. Nothing to keep me here.' He thought of Louise and knew that wasn't strictly true.

Brody mounted his new horse and set off through the town. He had only been there five weeks, but it seemed like half a lifetime.

He rode past the sheriff's office, which somehow looked different now that Will Tasker was no longer there. As he went by, acting sheriff Mikey stood in the doorway, waving to him.

'So long, Brody,' he shouted.

Brody slowed, and rode over in Mikey's direction.

'Are you settling in as sheriff then, Michael?' he said.

'Thanks to you. I don't know if my appointment will be made permanent.'

'I think it will. I'm sure that nobody will stand against you. Good luck to you.'

'And to you, Brody.'

Brody turned, and rode off down the street. As he rode past the theatre, he saw Louise watching from a window. He blew her a kiss. Through the closed window, he saw her speaking, but couldn't hear it. He could tell, though, that she was saying, 'Come back soon.'

He wasn't sure where he was headed. Texas, maybe, or California. He also wondered about Ishmael, the strange, educated outlaw. Even though the man was a thief and a murderer, Brody felt a sneaking regard from him, and suspected that he hadn't seen the last of him.

He took one look back at the window where Louise had been standing, saw that she was still watching him, then turned and rode on.